The Swimmer and Others

Michael McGrorty

ISBN 9781707959440

The Swimmer   Michael McGrorty

Inside the dark conning tower, I felt the bulkhead lurch as we left calm deep waters for the surface of the sea. The hatch hissed open at once, just as in the drills. The sky was black velvet except for a canopy of stars that swung gently above the outline of the town beyond the harbor. I felt my hands pull on the hard rubber fins, heard the hatch close behind me, and waited for the submarine to slip away.

The night was warm and the water tolerable. I took a last look at the outline of the buildings and glanced at my watch: It was just after midnight. The radium numbers of the compass on my arm glowed enough to be seen underwater. I turned toward 310 degrees, took the snorkel tube in my mouth, and began swimming just under the surface.

I was a thin and not particularly athletic child, prone to colds and sore throats. I was so weakened after a bout of Rheumatic Fever that my father put me in swimming lessons. My instructor was Miss Schantz, an older woman who had overcome polio by strengthening herself in the pool. She probably never had a worse student. At age ten I was nearly as uncoordinated as any victim of infantile paralysis. She spent weeks trying to teach me the side stroke, but never lost patience—though I hoped she would so I could go home. Eventually I learned to maneuver fairly well, but we came to an agreement that my stroke inventory would end with the side stroke and the crawl. The rest required too much communication between parts of my body that were not on speaking terms.

When my time with Miss Schantz was over, I figured I'd done with the pool, but my father insisted that I attend four days, every week. So, I went into the water to make unhappy waves. I had a habit of counting everything I did—sometimes aloud, to the discomfiture of my family. Thus, I knew the number of 25-yard laps I swam; the number of strokes to each lap; the number of breaths to each turn; and even the leg kicks it took to make up any distance. These numbers fell as my conditioning improved. It might be said that I kept at swimming for no other reason than to see how low I could get my stroke count. I was never interested in competitive swimming, and resisted all attempts to engage me thus. All I wanted to do was go back and forth in the water, counting strokes and kicks, with nobody to bother me.

There was a light chop when I began, and I heard the sound of waves scouring the line of the breakwater that barred the direct route to my goal. Its granite shards and boulders were covered in razor-sharp mussels, that delicacy of Mediterranean waters. After a few hundred strokes I felt a lifting surge with each wave, and knew I was close to those rocks. Atop them was a macadam path that might be patrolled, and which was certainly in clear view from the shore. The plan was to follow the line of the breakwater, concealed by its bulk, before turning at its end. I frogged along, keeping the back of my loaded vest as low as possible. After a small piece of time I heard a rhythmic double-slap, as though the waves had been caught in a corner.

At the origin of that sound lay a staircase descending from the macadam which had not shown up on the reconnaissance photos—probably because they were taken at high tide. This called for some thought. It might be a place where the Germans had placed an additional watch, from fear of sabotage; it might just be something the Italians had built to permit the landing of boats. The plan— that well-thought-out set of considerations put together by people who had never been in this position, told me to forget the staircase and keep going along the breakwater. But the breakwater path was hundreds more strokes to its end, a place where a steel net barrier waited to be breached, with only my hands and a small cutting tool. I stole a glance at the staircase and the rocks and the star-pricked sky. It was dark as it would ever get to be. I let a surge lift me onto the staircase, pulled off my fins and crept upward to see what might lie above.

I finished high school and got a soft job clerking in the Philadelphia Naval Shipyard. That December we got involved in the war, and I registered for the draft. I was sure they wouldn't take me because of the rheumatic fever, which was an automatic exemption. Two weeks after my physical I was marching at Great Lakes. After boot camp I went to school to become a clerk. Off-duty, I lifeguarded at the base pool. One afternoon some guy wearing Commander's stripes came around, summoned a bunch of us and said "Who here can swim the length of this pool underwater?" The others tried; some managed one length. I reached the end, turned back and made it to the start without a breath. A year later, give or take, I was riding a submarine to some place along the Adriatic coast where an American's life wouldn't be worth a fistful of lire.

There were twenty stone steps rising from the waterline to the edge of the macadam atop the breakwater, each about a foot high and half again deep. The steps were free of barnacles, which meant the path was important—for something. Snorkel in hand, I stole a look over the last step and scanned the length of the breakwater. I was about in the middle. It was too dark to see the watchtower or the marker pole at the far end. I couldn't have seen another person at twenty feet. This was good, because it meant nobody could see me. I crawled across the rough concrete to a matching set of steps descending to the calm, flat waters on the opposite side. Risky waters they were: without the ocean's chop, they would show the path of a swimmer clear as day. I might have stopped right there—gone back and followed the outside of the breakwater to the end and the turning—but for something that got into me a few days prior.

Far to the south, on a sandy spit of North Africa, where they taught a small cadre of swimmers to pursue the clandestine goals of the U.S. Navy, we were put to dealing with the sort of obstacles we would face on the job. Among these was netting. Netting could be made of ordinary rope, chain, or steel cable. It was all intended to keep something out: mainly ships and submarines, but also swimmers. Netting was tough to deal with. We were taught to cut it by one or another means so as to permit entry. But the enemy had no intention of standing by while we did this. They wired the netting, and topped it with buoys and flags; in any event, they knew exactly where it was and would usually know if it had been messed with. To play with netting was to risk detection, which devalued one's chances to something less than a handful of lire. Of course, there was doctrine, and teaching, and orders. But there was also that strong strain of feeling known known as the desire for survival, and moreover, the counterweight of experience. Not so much the experience of working with netting, but a particular feeling—call it an attitude—which accrued from other events.

The latter part of my training took place at a spot whose Arabic name was unpronounceable; the Germans called it something else, and it was, being distinguished by nothing more than a nice ocean view and hordes of biting flies. The Nazis left behind a trio of bombed-out ships in the harbor which it was supposed would make good play for navy divers. We learned mostly to identify the resident fish, some of which were edible. The nearby village was more educational. It taught many a sailor how to get the clap, and how to get his wallet lifted by the local urchins, the apparent support of invisible parents.

There was, inevitably, a small joint which functioned as the town watering hole. In the evenings sailors of low rank would assemble there to watch the sun quit the landscape, and to drink watered liquor, mainly Italian grappa, which needed all the watering it could get. One went outdoors to use the can. I was outdoors using the can when I heard shouts, and saw a welter of townies besieging a pair of sailors. The sailors were outnumbered, and their opponents armed with clubs. One of the sailors, a stout fellow diver, took a whack from an Arab, but seized his stick and whaled the tar out of him in the moonlight as his comrades fled. The victim turned out to be a person of some consequence, and the affair took on an ugly aspect. I was summoned before a tribunal to bear witness and thought the matter done, but it turned out that somebody in command had ordered that all concerned should be tossed in the brig. There being no brig for a thousand miles, I was informed that I was confined to quarters for the remainder of my time in that part of the world. This being the navy, the officer in charge cut me a deal: I could get out of my situation, and probably North Africa, if I were to volunteer to do some damage to a certain target which had proven invulnerable to previous efforts. It just happened to lie behind a set of steel cable nets.

The other two sailors were likewise permitted to try their luck against targets clothed in steel mesh armor. One perished in a Sicilian harbor when the metal curtain he was attempting to breach collapsed, with himself beneath; the other died when the wired mesh fence he was cutting in the harbor of Naples exploded in his face. I knew this because our radio friend, Axis Sally, was fond of revealing such details to discourage further adventures.

I did not desire for Sally to read my obituary to the whole of Europe, and I did not feel that I owed the navy my life to use in further experiments with wire mesh just because of a run-in with some Arabs, so, when the moment came, I slid my way across the rough macadam, hunkered down the concrete stairs on the other side, and slipped into the smooth water on the inner side of the harbor. There were no shouts; no gunfire; no flares—nothing but the sound of my own breathing and then the snorkel as I kicked my way along, two yards deep, surfacing only for another dose of air to continue the journey.

I saw the chart in my head, laid out in detail: seventy-five yards to the first pier; another fifty to the ends of the others, three in all, until a hundred-yard gap at whose end the object of my search would lie. With the pack I resembled a turtle, making shallow dives and resurfacing ahead—so many kicks until the next air, then a long exhalation and another deep breath. Fifteen breaths from the breakwater I rose and saw before me a barred block in the starlight: the first pier. I made for the end, skirted its pilings and went on, counting breaths and kicks to the next and the next. At the third pier I rose to check the space between myself and the quay wall, and saw the light: atop a cylinder beyond the water a yellowish-green dart of illumination stabbed the night. From the shadow of a piling I watched the beam lift and follow an invisible line to the end of the breakwater, light the rocks and macadam, then reach out to the start of the opposite line of rocks, washing their base, where it dipped and flared out. The beam was too steady to have been guided by hand. Its lamp had to be set in a template. Perhaps it was automatic. But that didn't mean there wasn't a man behind it, watching. The Nazis had a lot of men, even here on the Adriatic coast.

The searchlight had thrown enough shine to reveal the goal of my evening's work: a tapered steel box, fat as a sow, taking up 375 feet of quay wall and the attention of navies on both sides. She was the *San Blas*, a freighter that once plied a route from San Francisco to the ports of the eastern U.S. and Europe, carrying a general run of cargo. When the war began, she was running coffee from African ports to France and Italy. The conflict killed the trade, and the Fascists seized her to ferry troops. When her engines wore out the Germans set her on a quay, filled her with equipment and a crew to snoop on Allied radio traffic. They heard plenty and passed the word on to their superiors. They also jammed Allied channels and broadcast phony messages. Worst of all, they vectored Nazi planes to attack Allied ships and aircraft. The *San Blas* was trouble, and she had to go.

I knew that if there was anything on earth that was worth surrounding with a mesh spider web, it was the venerable *San Blas*. There would be no way to avoid the steel curtains, and all I had was an unfolding bolt cutter, a weak and cumbersome tool. But I also had a plan—one with no provision for the cutting of nets.

The reconnaissance shots showed submerged barriers surrounding the ship, beginning about 75 yards out, with another pair at 50 and 25 yards. The *San Blas* was stitched into place—she didn't need to go anywhere, so they put her in a steel corset and defied the world to undress her. But she was a nice old lady and I had no desire to steal her dignity.

I swam through the darkness, counting kicks until I knew I was a stone's throw from the first netting. At that point, blind but trusting, I took a couple of great deep breaths and dove to the bottom of the harbor. On the way I pulled out my torch lamp and pointed it downward. The floor had been gouged out to ten meters. My ears popped twice going down. I saw the sandy floor and kicked toward the ship again. Soon I saw the base of the net, secured to concrete blocks every few yards, and, as I'd hoped, full of gaps between large enough to pass a man. I rolled over, scrambled through the low arch below the first strand, and pushed on, ready to surface and take another lungful of air.

The trick was not to blow like a surfacing whale. One was taught to exhale gradually, then take in air slowly through the snorkel. I did just that, inhaled, and bent for the next dive. The next line of netting included insulated wires that would detect motion. I let myself drop to the seabed, shone my light along the base, but found no gap. Running out of breath, I lifted the first strand of the netting and found that it was attached to nothing—at least not where I was. Clear on the opposite side, I made for the surface and another dose of air. This left but one more fence to pass.

The third barrier was a latticework of concrete reinforcing rod, welded into a sort of cage supported by pilings. Its quality suggested hasty construction. I looked for joints rotted by salt water corrosion, and found that the frames were ragged where they rested on each other. It was no problem to force a gap in this basket; the challenge was doing it without making any noise and holding my breath. It took me a couple of tries, during which I barely succeeded in suppressing a paralyzing terror, before the fence bent enough for me to pass through.

I had no idea what might await me after that. I knew there was a ship somewhere in the murky darkness. It turned out there was nothing between me and *San Blas* but a few yards of oily water. I grabbed a breath beside her and descended for a trip beneath. She was thick and wide, but with no cargo aboard she drew only about fifteen feet. Her bottom was round as a salad bowl, and the Nazis kept it clean. On the other side were a set of fenders, nearly awash, which groaned and squeaked faintly as they rubbed against the quay and the hull. I surfaced beyond the end of one but saw nothing but a block of spangled sky before heading down to the job I'd come to do.

I heard every sound common to ships but that of running engines. Liquids flowed through pipes; various knocks and thumps indicated human activity. I wondered how many men were on duty aboard the *San Blas* that night. At least fifty. The rest would be sleeping.

Midway down the line of the keel, just to the port side, would lay a sea chest, where ocean water once entered to feed the boilers. My lamp found a grating about half an arm's span wide. That would be it. I rose for another breath, then descended, unbuckling my turtle's shell on the way downward. I held the lamp in my teeth, and followed the drill: *Turn the casing over so that its magnetic feet face the hull. Gently set the feet on the steel plating, making sure your hand is not between them and the metal surface. Turn the arming dial to its maximum setting.*

With that I kicked out, stole a breath and made for the first barrier.

I found the gap right away, which was greatly relieving. I didn't want to maintain an acquaintance with the *San Blas* longer than necessary.

I cleared the second gap in good time and then went under the third. All the while I tried to suppress panic, but didn't do a complete job. With duty behind me, I had only survival to pursue. I was no longer in the service of my country but a kid who just wanted to get home alive. When I hit the last pier, I rose for breath and found the harbor had come alive with noise and streaks of brightness. *I was discovered.* Hard spears of daylight jabbed angrily about, probing the piers and the water. Behind me on the road to the quay, an automobile prowled, headlights uncovered. This was Authority, arrived to make a Command Decision.

I heard a small engine sputter to life. That would mean a boat; likely more than one. Boats with lights and men with guns.

It would be futile to swim through the harbor to the breakwater. They would only shoot me like a carp in a carnival pond. The name on my dog tags would be chuckled out by Axis Sally, and a few people in North Philadelphia would grieve. There was no mention of problems like this in the training manual, and nothing to lose, so I decided to get out of the water.

Any set of piers has between them an access ladder for boats to tie up. I swam hidden between pilings until reaching a rocky wall at the pier head, then turned sideways. In twenty-three kicks I found a thick iron mooring ring, and above that, a ladder. The flashlamps were spearing hungrily, but none came in my direction as I climbed the sixteen rungs from the water's edge to the roadway. I hid behind a sandbag barrier, tucked fins and snorkel into my belt behind, then set off at a trot toward the breakwater and the open sea.

The big searchlight fingered the waters between the *San Blas* and the breakwater. It examined the heads of the piers, but was blocked by a succession of sheds lining the roadway. I knew I couldn't make it to the sea in the open, but might have a chance if I could jump along in the shadow of those buildings.

It was a hundred and four strides to the first shed, a corrugated hut with a broken door. Inside were coils of wire and a choir of squeaking rats. I stayed long enough to see the search light stab past on its circuit round the harbor, then raced seventy-six strides to the next shed, avoiding the inquisitive lamp again, and then again, across an open space of 80 strides, to a shed made of sheet steel. A pair of boats churned the waters beyond the piers. In the bow of each was a man with a bright lamp, and beside him, another with a rifle. Beyond where I stood there were no more sheds, but a very long stretch of open roadway that curved until it became the macadam path atop the breakwater. I could outrun any man who might pursue me to the sea, but not the searchlight, to say nothing of the guns on the search boats.

At that moment I recalled one of our lessons from the manual: *In your missions seek to follow the plan, but if this breaks down, remember that the enemy will be bound by his own plan and habits.*

I looked at my watch: it was fourteen minutes since I'd left the *San Blas*. I decided to start down the road toward the sea. A very unsafe plan, but the only one I had. I waited for the search light to pass again, took a deep diver's breath, and ran for the breakwater.

A hundred strides later my legs began to cast long, wiggling shadows. It was not the searchlight but the headlamps of an automobile. There was nowhere to hide. I was caught in the open. It occurred to me that saboteurs were invariably shot. I wondered what my last thought should be. A dark Italian sedan passed slowly, and stopped. A hatless officer in a grey raincoat emerged and thrust out his hand, saying "Bist du der Schwimmer?" I knelt, felt for the dagger at my calf, and rising, thrust it hard into the center of his chest. He bounced back on his heels, gurgled, and fell silent against the car. I said to the night, "Yes, my friend. I am the swimmer." The adrenalin in my veins made him light as a feather as I tossed his body onto the back seat.

The car had three forward gears and I used the lowest, driving slowly so as to resemble a Nazi intelligence officer looking for an intruder rather than a scared kid trying to get to safety. At that moment it came to me: *the Germans had their own swimmers.* The dead man behind me thought I was one of them, come to seek out the invader.

It might have been a furlong to the edge of the breakwater, but it seemed like the distance to the moon. When the curve became macadam, I looked for a place to start swimming. Seeing none, I thought it best to chance the rocks—my silent comrade might have friends approaching behind and I was running out of time for the rendezvous. My fins were on and I was waiting for a gap between surges when the granite rocks beneath me shifted.

Just before that moment, not a quarter-mile behind, a notch set in watchwork gearing passed the edge of a polished steel rod, the whole of that no bigger than your thumbnail. The rod shot through the notch and pushed a pawl sideways, closing a circuit. With that the process became a thing of chemistry. In a ten-thousandth of a second, my gift to the *San Blas* changed from a torpid putty to a fury of heat and gas.

The sea chest vanished, vaporized into its constituent atoms, which blew a wild gale through shattered bulkheads, boilers, and ventilation ducts. In the first quarter-second the engine room was devastated; in the next, the unmeasurable heat of new-born gases melted through the decks above. Before a full second passed, the hot storm reached the cool air of evening beyond the main deck, casting before it piping, metalwork, and the mangled remnants of the engines. In that same instant fire blasted forward and aft, flashing compartments to white heat. Men were incinerated before they heard an explosion. Moments later, its keel broken by the blast, the *San Blas* settled to the harbor floor, remains awash in flame and sparks.

I saw none of that. There was a flash behind me, but with it came a shock wave that threw me past the breakwater into the sea. My body skipped twice like a flat stone, and I landed face-down, somehow clad in fins, snorkel in hand. Instinctively I dove, which was fortunate, because in a few seconds, hot angry chunks of the *San Blas* began raining down. It was a good time to be underwater.

The opposite of 310 degrees is 130 degrees, southeast. I followed for two hundred kicks, which were much easier unburdened. I found my metal cricket, made a bit of noise, and cringed—beneath the water it sounded like a rifle firing. A hundred kicks further I did the same. Rising for breath, I scanned the horizon, aglow from the fire behind. I saw nothing else, felt nothing else. I didn't want to imagine that my friends had been frightened off by a Nazi patrol boat. I prayed there would be one—soon.

Before I could dive again a wave caught me, not from the direction of the swell but sidelong, and I slipped downward to avoid the wash. Not two yards down I struck bottom. But there was no gravel or sand. I'd hit the hull of a submarine. My submarine. Which, obedient to my signal, had made silent way to the place of the summons. Its conning tower rose; I climbed the inset ladder, then descended to safety and life. The last I saw of Italy was a bright flare on a black horizon, surrounded by searchlights and stars.

The Bugler   Michael McGrorty

T he bugle is an odd instrument. It has only five notes, and no valves. Every noise it makes has to come out of your own mouth. The bugle is also a lonely instrument. Nobody takes one to a party to show off. Its only place in the world is to start horse races, fox hunts, and the army.

In the summer of 1947, my job was to start the army every day on a base midway approximately between Lubbock and the center of the earth. Every morning I was escorted to the margin of a dark parade ground, to await the signal to begin playing *Reveille* as a sergeant raised the colors on a mile-high flagpole. In the evening I would play *Retreat* as the same sergeant yanked the colors down. Do that for a while and you get good at it.

Actually, I was pretty good before I started. Somebody found out that I could play the trumpet, so I spent most of boot camp marching with a horn. I hoped to spend the war in the States, but they needed replacements in Europe. I left for Germany, arriving late in '44, and was put to typing in a headquarters company. Six weeks before the war ended we took Frankfurt. The tanks rolled on but I was left to write reports and drive a colonel around the remains of the city.

Reveille is exactly 27 seconds long. You take a breath and start blowing; the idea is to make it crisp and seamless. An expert will make it sound like a cornet or trumpet rather than a scrap of brass tubing with a flared end.

I would blow *Reveille* on those Texas mornings, execute a sharp about-face and follow my escort to the roadway, where a deep-green army bus waited. I went in first, sat in an empty seat, and had my ankles shackled to a ring in the steel-plate flooring. With that our driver pulled away, heading in whatever direction we needed to go. Our destination was generally within a hundred-fifty miles, and usually closer. That part of the world is cotton country. There was nothing much to see except flat sections of dirt, which developed green sprouts that became tall woody lines of vegetation exploding with white lint five months later, when the harvesting machines would come, suck away the fiber, and leave the fields to another Texas winter.

There were little towns where the roads intersected, and near some of them, graveyards. Some of these were just plots graded out of the prairie scrub, their earliest graves unmarked, the board plinth having blown away in some spring tempest. The newer graves bore stone markers, many with the emblems of the armed services, for the war had sent its own harvest to the cotton country.

Our squat little bus would arrive before the services. Our escort, a not-particularly amiable buck sergeant named Clayton, would unlock the leg shackles of his four charges, who would then change clothing, concealed by the blacked-out windows in the rear of the bus. Depending on the order of the day, we could emerge as an army color guard, navy sailors, or any combination thereof. When this transformation was complete, we would emerge from the bus: two men carrying flags; one with a snare drum, and myself, bugle in hand.

By this time the assembly would have been given whatever speech or invocation was planned. Our job was simple: Clayton would bark out commands, and we would march. At the designated spot we would halt; the drummer and I would take places, the flag-bearers would dip their standards, and all of us would wait, casting a silent stare of attention over the landscape.

My drummer was Johnny Trent, a negro from Louisville Kentucky who tuned his snare as if it were a jazz band instrument. You'd expect a military rattle like a can full of stones, but Johnny's would come on in a slick sizzle, as though he were backing a combo and just waiting for his solo on the brushes. He was funny. After about five seconds of snare he'd give the slightest nod to me to begin playing. It was all I could do not to laugh.

Johnny only had two jobs in his life. One of them was the army. The other was playing drums in various Louisville bands, though he got as far away as Chicago if he could get booking. Gas rationing killed everything but the local gigs and the draft captured him before he could execute his plan of playing in clubs along the Mexican coast. He was working without enthusiasm in an English shipping depot when the front moved forward after the invasion of France. In about two drumbeats he discovered Paris, and shortly after that, an underworld of musicians who could and would hide and support a hot drummer who played like Chick Webb and who wasn't particular about pay, as long as he got somewhere to live. Paris is a large city and Johnny Trent vanished into it like a wraith, emerging after dark, playing all night, sleeping all day, living like there was no tomorrow.

He told me "I was doing two gigs—one in Pigalle—a hotel that was sort of a brothel. Members only, but with guests. Had a pretty good band there; four horns, three reeds, a pianist and me. There was this one woman who'd double on the harp and violin. Made it sort of classy. Early evening we'd do some dance numbers, maybe from nine to ten. After that it got wild. They wanted American stuff and we give it to them. Leader was this cokey guy named Arnie who didn't know a thing about music. He just come out, called the tune, made a few gestures and left the stand. We blew like hell. That would end about midnight so the customers could bed down. After that I'd be over at this basement joint, the Kansas City. It was supposed to be a little Cotton Club and they wanted it to be all 'jungle,' but not a black face on the premises except the band. I knew all Ellington's stuff and could do Sonny Greer's cymbal routines—that Chinese sound he got—and all the rim shots and stick twirls. They couldn't get enough of that. The first place I got paid fifty dollars a week. At the KC, I got that much and more. I tell you, it was heaven. They treated me like a man there."

Heaven went on for about a year. One evening he was approached by a stout Frenchman with a pock-marked face, who demanded a payment in order that he might become protected from arrest. Johnny told him to go to hell. The next night he was yanked from the bandstand by a brace of army MPs. He was charged with desertion, informed that he could be shot, and shipped to French stockade along with a few hundred others. Soon the stockade had become home to many thousands more— deserters gleaned from the streets of Europe, some of them criminals, others just fellows who had enough of the army and didn't want to go into, or back to, the war.

The army hadn't planned to deal with all that. If a man pled not guilty, he was entitled to a court martial, with an adequate defense, all of which could take weeks. Meanwhile the war effort was winding down and with it, the staffing to handle such affairs. After almost a hundred days of waiting, Johnny Trent was put on a troop transport and sent to the states, "case pending resolution."

I know because I was with him. The segregation that prevailed in the army then didn't apply to prisoners. We were stuffed, four to a two-person room, in a battered cruise liner whose last profitable runs had been made between Havana and Key West. We landed in New York and were sent by train to a tour of backwoods America.

At last, the train chugged into Texas, passed through a million miles of nowhere, and dropped us off in the middle of a hot night in a place whose tiny station sign read "Snyder." Which as it turned out, was about midway between Dermott and Hermleigh. The lot of us were cuffed like murderers and escorted to an open truck, which bumped on its springs through the darkness along a mostly dirt road until we reached the line of a hurricane fence which marked the edge of an army base. This was Morrison Depot, created as an assembly spot for armor being shipped to Fort Bliss and other places. Now they were processing tanks in reverse, mothballing them for future wars.

I thought we were going to be put into a prison, but the authorities hadn't planned for that, either. Instead we were bunked in ordinary barracks, albeit to ourselves. There were three dozen of us there, give or take. For a few days they put me to painting cosmoline on unused engine blocks, but then a lieutenant came around and said "I see that you can play the horn."

Taps is very different from *Reveille*. For one thing, it's slower. Slow is not a thing the bugle was meant for. *Taps* is about sixty seconds, and it's a real test of note-holding. Aside from that, nobody really hears you play *Reveille*. They're all practically asleep, and you're far away under a flagpole. You play *Taps* about ten feet from your audience. Do it right and you'll make them cry. I made them cry.

Part of the beauty of a military memorial service is the dignity and detachment of the honor guard and musicians. After *Taps*, we executed an about-face, marched together to the dark green bus, climbed aboard, and departed. The families and friends saw the army or navy give its grateful farewell and then disappear forever. The widows clutched their folded flags and our little group rolled away, newly shackled, to the next memorial service amidst the cotton fields of Texas.

One of our flag-bearers was a boy named Jamie Hardy who hailed from Seattle. Corporal Hardy was assigned to collect and inventory German pistols and rifles taken from captured troops. Before long he amassed a warehouse of Lugers and similar items. Pressure was brought upon him to part with these articles, especially by higher-ranking officers. Corporal Hardy succumbed to this pressure, but figured that if he were going to go bad, at least he might make some money off the enterprise. He made a little money before a disgruntled Luger-seeker turned him in to the authorities. Corporal Hardy was no genius, but he wasn't a fool. His last statement to interrogators was "If you take me down, I've got the names of a hundred officers, some of 'em Generals, who got guns from me." Hardy also opted for a formal court-martial, which was delayed several times, until at last he found himself riding a train for Texas.

The other flag boy was a very quiet lad named Paul Kerry who I believe was from somewhere in Ohio. He was working as a cook far behind the lines when the Germans made their last offensive push through the Ardennes Forest in the winter of 1944. He and many others were thrown into action against crack German units. Like many of the new defenders, Kerry hadn't fired a rifle since boot camp. Kerry and his company were pinned down and overrun. Captured and led away to a German encampment, he was interrogated by an officer who asked him "What do you do?" He replied "I cook." The Germans put him to gathering firewood, and eventually, to cooking their food. After two weeks the Germans were themselves overrun. When the G.I.s came through, they found Private Kerry standing in a dugout, preparing potato soup for a company that would never return. They asked him why he did it and he said "I cook." This was taken as a sort of confession, and the private was charged with aiding the enemy, there being no specific prohibition against making soup. He spent a good amount of time behind the wire in France before boarding a transport ship and then the trains that would take him to the plains of Texas.

On the twentieth of September, 1946, after having made a few people cry at a cemetery somewhere east of Acuff, our little caravan headed north, meeting Highway 62 and turning west. We stopped at Idalou for gas, our sergeant cranking the pump before going inside to pick up some sodas. The sergeant used to let one of us buy the cokes, but that was before what became known as The Rotan Incident.

On an April day of that year we set out for a set of five services, trying to make schedule despite the wide spread of our appointments across the map. We finished two, but lost two more to thunderstorms, so the sergeant decided that we'd just go for one that was indoors at a veterans' hall, outside the town of Rotan, then head home for the day. The ceremonies at the hall went off and we were standing outside the bus, waiting for our sergeant to open the bus door so we could sit down. But the sergeant discovered that the ceremonies provided refreshments, including a keg of beer. This being the case, he figured to toss down a couple of cold ones while we sweltered outside.

We were there a while when Pvt. Trent decided that we should just get on the bus and out of the sun. He pushed apart the folding doors and we got comfortable. Some time passed. We could see the sergeant inside, drinking his beer while holding forth with some of the local ladies. The effrontery of this inspired me to go for a nice lonely cornet that lay wrapped in a roll of oiled canvas in the back of the bus. In a moment I was blasting out *I Can't Get Started* with Pvt. Trent doing the rolls vigilantly just behind me. We went through several choruses before our sergeant arrived on the scene. He was unhappy and disappointed. We were to have our Good Time credits taken away. We would be thrown, all together, into solitary confinement. When he was finished, Pvt. Trent inquired "And what's to happen to you when we tell them you was drinkin' beer on duty?" The sergeant said nothing, but we were seldom permitted outside the bus unsupervised thereafter. On the way home that evening, Corporal Hardy said, quite without permission, "I didn't even know we got any Good Time credits."

When the sergeant returned with our Cokes, he said to us "We got one more play and then home."

I had an aunt who made me promise her two things on my tenth birthday: that I would never steal, and that I would learn to use a typewriter. In order that I wouldn't steal, she would give me a dime each Sunday when she arrived for supper. I took my first typing class in 8th grade. By that time, my aunt was giving me a quarter a week not to rob banks. Every year my allowance went up a dime, and I kept signing up for typing classes. It helped that I was usually the only boy in a roomful of girls.

There were only two types of work for the army in postwar Frankfurt: patrolling the dusty streets or working for the brass in some capacity. Because of the skill my aunt required I was put to typing voluminous reports of one sort or another; usually civilian requests and complaints. Of these there were many.

There was no Frankfurt, per se. There was only a bomb-crushed central ruin surrounded by islands of habitable space. Civilization existed, though it certainly did not flourish. At the time, the benevolence of the Allies provided civilians with a daily intake of 1,000 calories; fifty percent of normal, merely enough to ensure slow starvation. Many surrendered German soldiers were living under worse conditions in huge prisoner pens where the food situation was worse.

The commonest complaint was not lack of food, but the lack of food for children. Every day I wrote down the pleas of Germans, nearly always women; I didn't need a translator to understand 'Meine Kinder hungern.' The other big complaint was the absence of cooking fuel. The Germans had long since given up the hope of receiving coal; by the spring of 1945 they were asking for wood to burn. Frankfurt, a city whose architecture dated to Medieval times, had returned to the Middle Ages. Its citizens were put to work demolishing ruined buildings. They formed long caterpillars whose head gnawed gnawing at the remains of some structure, while the body passed back bits and chunks to be tossed into a pile by the roadside. Often a corpse would be discovered. This was tied to a stretcher and transported to the police station in a former park, where it would be identified and, like as not, burned along with the day's dead from malnourishment.

Our barracks were close to the office where I worked, but they were dark and depressing. The only alternative was a makeshift enlisted club where we were permitted to get as drunk as American beer could make us. After a few rounds of that I chose to spend my evenings completing reports.

I remember it was a Thursday evening; it had to be, because I was plowing through a stack of reports that had to be finished for the weekly meeting. My machine was an Underwood whose shift key read 'Umschalter' and backspace 'Rucktaste.' The clock told me it was nearly 21:00, and I figured to give it a few more minutes before turning in.

I heard the door open from the corridor with its usual squeak. I guessed that it would be some officer, come to fetch the keys he'd left behind, but it was only a cleaning lady. One bonus of being an Occupier was that you didn't have to mop your own floors.

I rolled a last sheet of bond paper into the bale, gave it a twist and started plinking. At the end of each line, I hit the return and started again, over and over. A good typist never looks at his machine, but one of my keys got caught in the cleft and I had to tap it out. That's when I caught sight of the cleaning lady. She was using a straw broom to sweep under the long line of desks that led to mine, using a figure-eight motion, keeping her pile of dust centered in the aisle. With the light behind she formed a silhouette, like a marionette who danced against a painted screen. She had the legs of a dancer, too: long and thin, with arms to match.

She was two desks away and bent down to brush dust onto a piece of cardboard. She finished, straightened herself, then pivoted and collapsed, falling in slow-motion to the wooden floor, her broom clapping against the boards. I rose quickly and put an arm beneath her shoulders. She was light as a cloud. For the first time I saw her face.

Her eyes were open but vacant. I thought she might be dying, but she suddenly the puppet came to life, sat up and said "I am fine. Just an accident." This was uttered in the perfect English that upper-class Germans are taught in school. I replied "Nobody's fine who falls down like that."

After a few moments I helped her to rise, and sat her down on a steno chair. Her hands were cold. When I grasped her arm it was like a hoe handle wrapped in suede. She said "I must finish now." I said "You're finished, now. Stay put while I make some tea."

I boiled a pot, poured her a mug and added a great portion of milk. She drank with trembling hands until the cup was drained twice. I found a slab of cobbler in the icebox and shared it with her.

When we finished I said "My name is Martin Bauer. I am from Madison, Wisconsin, which has many German residents."

She said "My name is Greta Bergen. I am from Frankfurt, which is no more. And now I must work."

It was nearly ten o'clock. Greta resumed her waltz with the straw broom and I thought to myself that I had never seen such a beautiful girl. She swept her way out of the office, never pausing to look in my direction. That night I fell asleep with her face emblazoned across my dreams, and especially her eyes; pale green and flecked with gold, like a brook in a summer sun.

The following day I endured six hours of meetings before retreating to the office for finish the week's paperwork. I reached in the top drawer for a piece of bond and began to type, saw typing on the back of the page:

Mister Bauer,

Please forgive my weakness last night. I was a bit light-headed. Probably I forgot to have my supper. You were most gracious and gentlemanly. There is a deficit of that quality these days—if that is the correct way to write this.

I have my job through the grace of God and the fact that I can speak and write English. I am glad that I was not assigned to the 'typing pool' in the other building because such seems to be merely a harem for the benefit of American military officers. Whatever you do, do not endanger my position. The wages are small but constant, and at present, all I have.

When you see what remains of Frankfurt you know the condition of my heart. There was once a beautiful city here, a place of art, history and culture. That is vanished forever. I was twice destroyed. The first time was when my father's clothing store was burned to ashes in the bombings of 1943. The second time was when the Stadtbibliothek was destroyed in 1944. That was more than a city library. I was a researcher there, writing a thesis on English views of Goethe. That was my work, and thus my life. Both of these have vanished as well, like my father's work and fortune, into dust and smoke. But I cannot let myself complain or fall prey to despair— look around you. There are thousands with no home and many whose families, whose priceless children, have died.

You are from Madison, Wisconsin. So, in a way, am I. Having relations in that area, I applied to study for a Doctorate at the University. The war wiped that hope away.

I know Americans well enough to realize that you will very likely attempt to speak with me again. I will accede to this wish on condition that you remain a gentleman, and with one other requirement: that you not put milk in my tea henceforth. If there is not a lemon for a thousand kilometers, I can wait for one.

G.B.

It was useless to attempt work after that. All I could do was wait for evening. At precisely 21:00 the side door to the office opened and in swept my German friend. She gave me no notice whatever, but danced along with her broom as if she were skating with a partner on a frozen pond. When she reached my desk and I said "For you," and handed her a small box wrapped in foil paper. Inside she found a lemon.

"Where did you get this?"

"Probably from Spain, via England. Americans never do without. Let's make some tea."

"No," she replied. "Not until ten. That's when I'm done."

She had it timed to the moment. At ten o'clock I had a pot of tea and two cups waiting, along with a strudel.

I asked if she would stay in Frankfurt.

"That isn't up to me. You know we aren't allowed to move about without permission."

"Would you move?"

"To where? This is my city. Even in ruin it is mine."

"Where are your parents?"

"They were killed in the bombings."

"I am sorry."

"Well, it is perhaps better. I loved them dearly but it would have destroyed them to see this place now."

There was a long silence and then I said "Can I take you home—I mean, to your house."

"I know what you meant. I learned vernacular English by the radio. I have a better idea. Let's go for a walk."

The evening was cool and very clear, with a full moon on the horizon. I said to her, "Lead the way," and we strolled off, out past the guard shack and into the streets of the city.

She said "I'm in a hostel they set up for single women just beyond the river. It's about a kilometer."

The main streets were clear of rubble, but here and there were the marker flags warning of unexploded ordinance. It seems as if the Allies dropped an equal proportion of duds to live bombs. In the car with my colonel I hadn't had to avoid these.

We approached the cathedral, whose tower stood out amidst the ruins like an accusing finger. Greta grasped my arm and said "Let me show you something."

She led me into the churchyard and then across to a stone wall. "This was the cathedral choir. Come with me—hold my hand, the ground is full of rocks."

We scrambled through a doorway into the choir, which was now a stone box, open to the sky. High above, a latticework of iron remained of the roof. We passed into the church proper, through a rubble of stone chunks, and found ourselves in a great columned emptiness whose outlines were marked by the moonlight.

Greta said "This was my church. I was here every Sunday—not so much to pray as to be in this beauty, with the souls of all those who came before."

She took me forward, saying "This was the altar. My parents were married on this spot."

A breeze came through the broken places, bringing with it the scent of dust and ashes. She grasped my hands in hers and said "What do you want from me, Mr. Bauer? I am only a girl in a ruined city. I have nothing left but dignity. Whatever you wish, don't take that away."

A tear coursed down her cheek and I kissed it away, and then kissed her mouth, and whispered "I only want to be with you—here or anywhere. I'll do anything to make that happen."

Before we could stay longer, she said "The doors to the hostel will close soon. Let's go now."

It was a short way to the hostel. I left her there and turned for home, passing the cathedral grounds once more. In the distance lay the broken span of the Alte Brucke, the oldest bridge on the Main. Beneath it passed the river, unconcerned, a sheet of hard silver in the moonlight.

My life from then became the meeting with Greta at ten every evening, followed by tea and our walk to the hostel. She wrote me letters and I wrote her back, using up the army's time and stationery, telling her of my plans for her and us. Whenever I got the chance I would re-read our sheaf of correspondence, unable to go more than a few hours without some bit of her.

It was another Thursday, not six weeks after our first tea, when the roof fell in. I was pulled from my bed and taken to the headquarters of the Military Police, where I was questioned by a Lieutenant who wore the insignia of the Judge Advocate Corps. They don't fool around in the army, and he got right to business.

"You are being charged with fraternization. The subject is a German national named Greta Bergen."

I thought he was the prosecutor, but it turned out he was my counsel. The prosecutor was less friendly, if that's possible. He gave me the usual options: plead guilty, or suffer a court martial and a dire sentence.

In the hallway of our office was placed a poster depicting victims of Nazi atrocities, with the warning 'Remember This! Don't Fraternize!' We were explicitly warned not to associate with German civilians—in speeches, in policies, in a set of rules that came with a perforated page we were expected to sign and which was placed in our personnel folder. Yet it happened. Just as it happened in France and Italy and England and everywhere else on earth where Americans set foot. We got friendly with the locals. Some of us got very friendly. As might be expected, enforcement lay heaviest upon the enlisted ranks. The affairs of officers, figuratively or otherwise, were either ignored, or if things got too sticky, the offender was sent to a distant command or permitted to resign his commission. But there were periodic crackdowns, and of course, nothing better than to make a few examples as a warning. My downfall occurred because my correspondence with Greta was discovered by a fellow G.I. who was snooping in my desk.

For twelve days I was 'confined to barracks,' instead of the stockade, and not really that, because my colonel insisted upon my company for his regular rounds, and for my typing, which was essential if his reports were to be submitted in good order. Nothing really changed. I saw Greta every weeknight at the same hour, then left her for my own barracks rather than escorting her home.

But I was in limbo. At some time, on some day I was to be sentenced for my crime; until then I would simply go on, waiting. I wrote to the prosecutor, asking to plead guilty, but he gave no reply. I was beginning to think that I'd be smelling the burnt remains of Frankfurt for years when, on a Sunday morning, I was grabbed by the M.P.s, hand-cuffed, and sent bouncing with a few other miscreants in an open truck to the port of Rotterdam, where we embarked for the United States.

I met Johnny Trent on that ship, and stayed with him to the last whistle-stop in Texas, to blow and rattle until the government damn well pleased. I wrote to Greta every day, but received no mail in return. I was starting to lose my mind when a lady from the Red Cross gave me a telegram which read:

MY LETTERS RETURN MARKED 'NO RELATION.' /
RECEIVE YOURS / NO LEMONS / LOVE GB

By which my life was restored.

Our last stop of the day was at a hilltop graveyard, a spot chosen because it was too stony for cotton. It must have been hell for the gravediggers. The age of the mourners suggested that they were burying a veteran of the Great War, or something earlier. We stopped the bus in the lee of the wind, made our entrance and gave them the routine. After that it was an hour's drive south. We hit the base gate at 16:00 and I was hoping to get some chow before the food ran out, but the sergeant said to his mirror, "The guard said to go to the AJ office for some files."

The bus pulled up to that office. An officer stepped out, said "Bauer," into the doors, and my sergeant released me from my shackles. Inside, a bored clerk handed me a folder with my name on the outside. He said "Read page one."

I was just starting to read when he added "Skip to the bottom. You sign that now, you're out of the army. Today."

That didn't hit me quite right and I said "What about the charges?"

"They're gone, Sport. No time to prosecute. Sign and you can go home."

I was too smart for that. "What kind of discharge?"

"Honorable. You get all the benefits. Look, hurry up, will you? I got others to do."

It was true. The army was going to pretend as if nothing had ever happened, probably because they didn't want to admit that nothing had. I signed the paper in black government ink, hand shaking, and was presented with a voucher for my pay, obtainable in the morning.

On my way out of the office I saw Johnny Trent. I didn't want to let him in on the secret, and brushed past into the street. The bus was waiting. Our sergeant said "Don't get all flustered up now. You got about ten minutes before colors."

Half a minute later a crazy black man jumped down the steps of the office, screaming something like my name amidst a storm of disconnected syllables. He managed to calm down enough on the drive to the flag pole so we could execute our business. The colors went down, *Retreat* was sounded, and Johnny Trent never sounded better. We opted to walk to the barracks. Johnny resumed his rejoicing. "God damn, we goin' now for sure! Let's get us some beer tonight. I ain't had none in months!"

We made that detour and had that beer. At the end of the night Johnny said to me "What you goin' to do first in the morning?"

"Go with you to the paymaster. Then to the telegraph office. Then the hell out of here." We laughed together and I added "Where are you headed, anyway?"

"I'm stopping in Louisville for a spell. After that, France. I'll ride that long as I can. What about you?"

"Madison. I got to see my folks. And I'm going to see about getting somebody here from Germany."

"Can you do that?"

"If I can't, I'll be on the boat with you."

Early next morning I awakened at the usual time and waited for the sound of *Reveille*. The bugler had a fair tone but was a bit slow. I got breakfast, then wired a hundred dollars to Greta with a message:

MAKE PLANS / GET YOURSELF SOME LEMONS /
MORE SOON / LOVE MARTIN.

The Crop-duster   Michael McGrorty

I n early 1945 we were chasing the Germans through France toward the
Rhine, using patched-up airfields for reconnaissance, bombing and
strafing. I was flying a P-47 and had been for the whole of my time over-
seas. I will say this: she was reliable and sturdy as the devil. People say she
was a heavy plane. Not for an airliner, but certainly for a machine intended
to duel it out with the Focke-Wulf or Messerschmitt. Her strong points
were toughness and firepower, but I was glad when they took us out of
escorting bombers and put us in the line of blasting ground targets.

The formula was simple: you got briefed, got into your plane, flew to
the designated area and shot the living hell out of a particular rail line,
depot, power station, or, if you were lucky, a convoy of German supply
trucks. The P-47 was a good tool for the job. She had eight fifty-caliber
machine guns in her wings, each of which would have been devastating
to anything but a tank or a concrete bunker. In combination they could
throw about twelve pounds of lead in a second. If that weren't enough, the
harder targets could be removed by bombs or rockets. My favorite load was
a pair of 500-pound high explosive bombs, but there were also missiles. I
hated those. Although they let you do your shooting at a safe distance, they
could wander off course. Your 500-pound TNT bomb only needed gravity
to do the job.

On any day in good weather we would be out there setting things afire.
Most of the time we did one mission, but it wasn't uncommon for us to be
sent out twice or even three times, depending on what was out there. From
about February of '45 through the end of March we were doing two a day,
with the second one about as welcome as a rock in your shoe.

They say crop dusting came along in the fifties, but that's just wrong.

Depending on where you were in the country, it had been going on since right after the First World War. I know because I did a lot of it.

My father was a seed salesman in East Louisiana. All that really means is that he was a wholesaler who stored seed until time to fill orders. One Spring day, when I was fifteen, one of his customers came in and said he'd started dropping rice seed from an airplane. We'd had a couple of really wet years and you can't drill it in when the ground is muddy. That means you wait, and waiting means you may not hit the good weather and your yield will be poor. So this guy had hired himself an airplane pilot to drop seed from the sky.

Now, my father was not the smartest guy in the county, but he knew how to chase a buck. He got in touch with this airplane driver, a former army guy named Gil Bland, and asked if he'd like to be supplied with rice seed, direct, to save on the whole deal. Mr. Bland agreed, and in short order I was delivering special "air-plane" rice to his shop over in Fenton. Like everything else in farming, seed is bought on credit. Mr. Bland had run up a nice bill with my father, who expected to be paid when the farmers paid Bland—after the harvest. This put Mr. Bland in the way of an obligation to my Dad, who never missed the chance to take advantage. He said "Why don't you take my son on to help you?" By which two birds would be killed: I would be out of his hair, and moreover, made to pay my own keep rather than eating out of his icebox.

Mr. Bland accepted the offer, and I was put to work. My first day began before sunrise. I was assigned to drive a flatbed loaded with my father's seed to a crossroads about ten miles distant, and to wait. I drove there in the early morning light, and waited. After a little while I heard a whine and sputter, and then saw, up close, my first aircraft. It was a Curtiss JN-4, one of many that the government sold off after the war. Of course I didn't know that at the time; to me it was just an airplane, miracle enough for that. I also didn't know that it was rather cropped in the wings, which had also been broadened for slow-speed stability. All of that knowledge came later.

Mr. Bland swept a low pass overhead, turned back into the wind and plopped the Jenny down smack in the middle of the oiled road. With the propeller turning, he jumped out and said "Grab me one of them bags and get over here." One does not exactly 'grab' a hundred-pound bag of rice, but I managed to get it over my shoulder and in the vicinity of the plane. Bland helped me into the plane's rear seat, buckled me down, and set the bag of seed on my legs like a blanket. He followed this with another, which about crushed me. When that was done he said "Okay Sport. There's a tin hopper right in front of you. It holds one bag of rice and it's full now. As it empties, pour more in. When I raise my arm, you pull on this cord. That lets the rice fall out. When you let go, it stops. When we're down to the painted line on the hopper, give me a shout and we'll go down for more. Got it?"

I nodded, he gunned the engine, and we sped off down the road. In a few seconds we lifted up, not so very far above the fields, made a turn, and began a run down a sodden black field. Bland lifted his arm; I yanked the cord; he waved; I let the cord go. We did this for maybe five two minutes before the hopper was empty, whereupon the Jenny was set down again, rolling to rest near the truck for another load.

We quit for lunch, sitting in the flatbed's cab together. He told me "This goes on for about a month, every day but Sunday. You stick with it and I'll teach you to fly one of these things."

Bland moved his operations northward with the warming spring, ending up in East Texas by the middle of April. By that time I had become his boon companion, surviving a couple of hard set-downs, two or three tongue-lashings, and a fight with some obstreperous drunks who wanted a free plane ride.

When the planting season ended, my boss moved back to the shop in Fenton, inviting me to stay there gratis. This was not so generous an offer as might seem. The accommodations consisted of a booth in the corner of a sheet-metal shed. Despite this I set myself down there. Why? Well, because Mr. Bland was not my father, and because he was connected to airplanes, and moreover, he had promised that I'd learn how to fly.

Thus I became the man-of-all-work—especially the oily kind. Bland was in the process of scavenging an entire engine out of a bunch of blown motors, and he needed me to assist this surgery. This work more or less cemented my desire to become a pilot rather than a mechanic. The engines were OX-5 V-8s, most with at least one cylinder shot. At the time these could be had for scrap prices; all one had to do was pay the man and be able to haul off a 350-pound lump of metal. Bland was not much of an engineer. He knew little more than how to put the thing together, and was lucky that the motor in question did not have very exacting tolerances.

He also had a stock of busted Jenny parts, hanging in pieces from the rafters of the shop. The plane was essentially a flying picnic basket, a spruce frame trussed in wires, altogether not very far advanced from the Wright Brothers' *Flyer*. It had the aerodynamics of a kite, and about as much control. With all that, it was very easy to operate. Between the pilot's legs rose a stick exactly like the handle of a baseball bat, and also a set of foot pedals, by which the machine was urged to do what little it could do to rise, turn, and avoid the ground until landing, which was more or less a planned collision with the earth. The problem with the Jenny was that she had none of what is known as 'directional stability.' She flew like a bird instead of an arrow, dodging, dipping, swinging this way and that every few seconds, even when the wind wasn't blowing—and much more so when it was. That being the case, when one mastered her moods and flaws, he could really be considered a pilot.

One day, when we were waiting on a delivery, Bland said to me, "I put the control stick on the rear cockpit. Let's go fly the Jenny." It was my sixteenth birthday. Bland took her into the air and then shouted "she's all yours." That was the extent of my instruction, but with Bland at the front controls, I knew I was relatively safe. He let me take her on a figure-eight around the county and then land her on the endless road adjacent to our property, so we would have enough dirt if I couldn't spot her down right away. But I did. And just as quickly he took her up again, to land nearer our shop.

He led me into the shop, opened up two bottles of beer, handed me one and said "In a few days I expect you to be ready to start riding this thing around."

Three years down the road, a man from the government came around in a dark green sedan and introduced himself to Bland, who didn't seem happy to meet him. After a few remarks, the stranger came to where I was varnishing some wooden struts and said "I'm George Blassingame, Department of the Army. How many hours you got in the air, solo?"

"Almost two thousand."

"Any single-wing?"

"About half of that."

"Okay, Son. We're looking for pilots. There's a war coming. You can either get drafted into the infantry or get into an airplane. You need me to talk to your folks?"

I decided that I didn't want to live in a tent, and my career with Mr. Bland ended shortly thereafter.

It was a Thursday, early in March. We got the assignment to cover 'zone 65,' a place about ten miles out of France, just over the Rhine. The Germans were building up reserves there to defend against our crossings and we were trying to ruin their plans with as much harassment as possible. I didn't like the sound of the order. Zone 65 contained a rail line and a paved road through which much equipment was made to travel—a sort of gauntlet run by day, when our planes were especially active. The two pathways ran out of a hilly forested area into a plain covered with farm fields—fodder, some grain, and potatoes. It was pretty country, but not a good place to be. To protect traffic, the Germans lined the roadway with antiaircraft guns, particularly the very nasty 37mm cannon. These were usually mounted on halftrack trucks, but we'd seen them stationary, and even on wooden wagons. They were easy to hide and tough to evade. They could reach up to about 14,000 feet, but they also were very good at shooting up low-flying planes because they could swing about quickly to intercept low-flyers—which is what we were going to be on that day. To add to this, every German soldier in the area could be expected to fire at us with whatever he had. In that theater, the odds of being hit by ground fire were about one in every twenty missions. The odds of being shot down were about one in every fifty. By that day in March I'd been hit by ground fire four times in fifty-four missions.

Gone were the days when we'd roll across the sweet acreage of the French countryside, hunting down locomotives and shooting up depots.

The Germans had quit running; moreover, they had run of out of room. Everything we shot at these days shot back.

At that phase of the war we were sending up one experienced pilot with two replacements. I was given two relatively green guys, Jim Morrows and Bill Curt. Together they probably had fewer flying hours than a housefly. Curt I liked: he was timid, but reliable. Morrows was something else. He wanted to win the war all by himself. He had trouble remembering orders, and was a poor formation flier. I think they put the two of them together to cancel out their shortcomings. They put them with me so I could teach them to fly, but it was a bit late in the game for that.

The routine was simple: take a zig-zag course through about twenty miles of France before hopping over the Rhine at about ten thousand feet; swing an arc around the known flak fields, then patrol our way through Zone 65, shooting at whatever looked good along the way.

We had breakfast, got our briefing, and I took my two kids aside for a chat. I told them "You heard the man in there. We're going to be shooting rockets today with no bomb load. I'll pick the targets and lead in. Curt, you follow; Morrows, you come up behind. Mind your spacing. I may not fire on the first pass. If I don't, hold your fire, and that means guns, too. We're getting a lot of decoys and I don't want to waste rockets. Fire your rockets on the 'instant' setting with the 'dual' toggle down. Fire only one salvo on each run unless it's a long train or railroad tracks—watch to see what I do. Aim down and remember 'rockets follow line of flight.' Got it?" They should have got it, after all the time they'd spent training. I think I only went over the routine to keep them from getting scared.

We got off at nine on the dot. The sun cast our shadows ahead and slightly to the right as we flew in a staggered line over newly-liberated country. At 300 miles per hour we were over the Rhine in fifteen minutes, where the real show began. I saw the first bank of Krupp eighty-eights flash from the point of a hilltop and led the others into a set of quick course changes to avoid the shells. At our altitude they had to calculate our course and speed, shooting ahead in the hope that we would simply run into their cloud of exploding rounds. The puffs of their explosions were visible, but none came close enough to hurt.

A minute after crossing the border I set us down lower and spread the group out. My turning point was the spire of a church set in a small valley. Something made me change my mind about this. I turned the group wide left of the steeple and watched as a legion of flak guns made frantic efforts to turn their barrels about. By the time they got untied we were far beyond reach.

At that point we were dragging our shadows like anglers trolling a pond. Farmsteads passed beneath us—places the war hadn't managed to ruin and wouldn't get a chance to. Here and there a cow wandered, a patch of brown cloth on a green carpet. The Germans were the neatest farmers on earth. Their barns never sagged and their fences were arrow-straight. It almost made you admire them until you remembered that most of those homesteads were being worked by slave laborers from Russia or Poland.

I didn't need the map to know that we were just west of the roadway and rail line. I yanked us up a bit higher for some perspective and saw their parallel lines running south-southwest through the farms, and occasional clumps of forest. A few seconds passed; three or four miles of track and road went by, and then I sighted what looked like a locomotive and a line of rail cars rolling toward us, smoke following the wind from its stack across the fresh fields. It seemed like a real train and not a Nazi decoy. There was no tunnel around for it to hide in, which meant I had time for a check before a return to launch rockets. A look in my mirror showed me that Curt was in position but Morrows had moved up to tailgate me. It was too late for a flying lesson so I just left the radio alone and began our check-out run.

I came down at a strafing angle, pretty flat, and found that, sure enough, we were looking at a real, live, coal-burning locomotive, probably pulling troops to the line to fight the Third Army. If history was any guide the soldiers would abandon the cars for the farm fields. But it didn't matter: it was the train I was after. We could strafe the soldiers all we wanted after that.

I remember my hand was on the stick, and we were not more than two hundred feet above the rail cars. If I'd been looking, I'd have seen a flash from Morrow's right pylon, and then another from the left, followed by streaks of flame. But I wasn't looking behind me just then.

What I saw was a streak of something speed from under my plane to strike the middle of the rail cars. I never saw the second rocket. The first one hit the cars, which erupted in a blast of metal and wooden shards. I was so close that the concussion, the spray of material, and the sound of the rocket's explosion arrived in the same moment. My plane, all five tons of her, jumped like a puppet on its strings, veered slightly toward the sun, and began to bleed—first oil, and then fire, from two places along the rim where her engine cowling used to be. The controls worked the plane, but the manifold pressure dropped like a dying man's pulse. I watched my air speed fell toward the stall point, swallowed hard and tried to get power to the engine.

Even through the smoke I could see we were short at least two of the eighteen cylinders in the radial arrangement. The others were dumbly consuming fuel as if nothing had happened, but then so were the ruined ones, which made for the smoke and spurts of flame. It seemed like an hour, but it might have been ten seconds before the ruined cylinders shed their pistons and connecting rods, which came past my canopy in red-hot globs before tumbling to the German countryside. With that the fires quit, though the smoke went on billowing.

Two things occurred to me: The plane was flying, and I hadn't any holes in my flight suit. I hit the radio but got only a long, unfriendly buzz of static. I set my aircraft into a slow turn to the east. There was no crash debris, but my two comrades had vanished. Morrows had jumped the gun, firing two rockets—in sequence rather than in pairs—which blasted the train and my aircraft. We were far too low and close for rockets. That's what my report would say, if I could get that plane out of Germany.

Which I was attempting to do when the remaining cylinders began to overheat, indicating a severed oil line, or a leak somewhere else. Even on a straight line, at that speed, I might not have enough motor left to make the border. I let the plane descend, which it had no inclination to resist—and looked for a spot to crash-land among the verdant farms, cranking down the landing gear just in case.

I saw a narrow lane, straight and good, along the edge of a large hay planting. The farmer would have used it to run his wagons after mowing.

But it was Spring now and the path lay empty. I was about a stone's throw above it when my airspeed went away and we smacked down on our wheels.

It was not a textbook landing. The earth captured us and then tried to give us back to the sky, which protested and tossed us down again. This exchange went on for the longest minute of my life, ending in a draw, a skid, and a squeal of brake linings. Behind me lay a pair of shallow grooves sliced in the road; ahead of me lay more dirt pathway, hay on either side, and blue sky above.

There was a lot of war going on in that country, but none where I was. Even so, there were many witnesses to the attack. That might not bring a patrol plane—the Germans hadn't very many—but it would bring soldiers, homing in on the spot where the observers saw the smoke from the rocket blasts. I was fairly distant from there now, but not terribly far, and a grounded fighter plane tends to catch the eye. I considered the possibilities: the better outcome would be capture; the lesser one a bullet. At that stage of the war, the Germans did not go easy with invaders on their turf. My personal defenses consisted of a dull knife and an aluminum revolver of unknown reliability.

My watch told me it was 9:45 in the morning. Most of the farms around me were small holdings whose owners would have been up for an hour before sunrise. Certainly they would have seen me land. About now they would be talking to each other—not by phone, because we had shot the lines to hell, but over fences and in the fields.

I climbed down and made a close check of my vehicle. The underside of the plane was scorched black in a pattern of sooty swirls. The wings and fuselage had a total of thirty-six holes blown in them, most about the size of a half-dollar. I pulled a warm bit of steel from one perforation—it was from a bomb casing. If nothing else, we stopped at least one delivery of ammunition from reaching the front. There were no leaks that I could see.

Back of the engine were two long trails from burnt oil, each leading to a ruined cylinder. The two lost cylinders left gaps like the missing teeth of a street fighter; their housings were gone and everything inside was somewhere behind me on the fresh fields of the Rhineland. The engine stood out naked, with only a ragged root of its cowling attached behind. The props were nicked here and there, but not loose. Nothing leaked—whatever lines had been cut had either healed themselves or run out of fluid. The air stank of hot oil and the cooling fins ticked as they lost heat.

I climbed back inside and checked my radio, but got nothing but noise. I was barking my callsign into the mike when I heard a thump somewhere below me, and then another. I climbed down and found a middle-aged man standing over a bicycle at the rear of my fuselage. He said to me "Did your supercharger go, or was it the cylinders?"

For some reason I said "Go up front and see. And by the way, who are you?"

"Never mind who I am, Captain Dennis. What matters now is getting you off this road before the Luftwaffe comes around."

He rolled forward and examined the engine. "Okay," he said. "You have a couple of oil lines that need plugging. That and the fuel tubes."

If he was a German, he didn't sound much like one. I said "So you are from where?"

"As far as you need to know, I am from Shangri-La. Jump down and come with me."

Having no other reasonable option, I complied. He shook my hand and said "John Mueller. That's good enough for now."

"How did you know my name?"

"The same way I knew that your junior partner, Lt. Morrows, botched your little raid."

"You monitor our radio traffic."

"Yes, but we know what you plan to do every day, and of course we see you fly over, too."

I was about to say something but heard a noise behind us and turned to look. It was a four-mule team being led by a man in a straw hat. I said to Mueller, "Pretty good stock."

He shrugged. "French, with French attitudes."

The team clopped along, passing us and coming to a halt on the command of its driver, who spoke French to his charges.

I said "Let me guess—you plan to drag this plane somewhere."

"No—they do. I plan to go with you to my house."

At that point I wouldn't have been shocked to find that he intended to tow the plane to the moon. And so I went away with a complete stranger who gave me a phony name but who knew exactly who I was and what business I was about. I did this because I had no alternative, and because I was by that point burning to find out what the hell exactly was going on.

Mueller took me down the road a bit deeper into Germany, and then we made a sharp turn toward a stone house not far off. It was obviously a farmer's residence, with its main stock barn close by and stacked hay forming a half-circle to the north.

"Your family home?" I asked.

"Yes and no," he replied.

I realized how silly I must look, staggering along in my pilot's suit, but that fit with the rest of the situation. The fields surrounding the house were sprouting tufts of dark green leafy vegetation. I took a walk to one of the rows and yanked up a very large turnip.

"We call those 'Steckrube.' Means 'Swedish turnip.' The English just call them 'Swedes.'" They're for pigs, cattle and horses, but these days they fetch a better price as human food. You can graze horses on them and the roots remain, but pigs root them right up."

"We don't do that in Louisiana."

"You couldn't. Too hot. They like the cooler weather here."

"How much land you got in these?"

"You would say—what—'half a section.' About 320 acres. The rest is in grass and potatoes, alternating. Dry-land farm, six square miles, both sides of that dirt road."

"How'd you learn farming?"

"My father raised me here. But I got out of the middle ages by going to America for college. Cornell University, Agriculture and Botany. Married a local girl, brought her here, had kids."

"Are they inside?"

"They are inside of a nice farm in Kentucky right now, and have been for a while. A little exchange I made for their safety."

Instead of taking me to the house, we went over to the barn. He was a farmer, all right. It was a good-sized, split-level stone-and-wood affair, something like the ones in New England, but with a higher roof. There were stalls for the draft horses to one side; stacked fodder and feed on the other, and a plain lumber floor beneath all.

He said "I keep the tractors in a storage out beyond here. Can't get enough petrol to use them anyway. This floor is maybe twenty meters by twenty-five."

"Large enough for a hangar."

"It will be."

"You don't mean to bring that thing in here? Why?"

"Get it out of sight. Maybe do some repairs. My friend, you are my biggest problem right now. I have to get rid of that plane, and the best way I can do it is by having you fly it away."

That made sense, if only in the bizarre way that events had turned logic inside out. Mueller said "Let's go into the loft."

It wasn't much different than any hayloft I'd ever been in. There was even a cat present, licking its wrist on a cube of fodder. Mueller said "We have a hay-lift. Much better than block and tackle. Something I learned in America." I bent over and looked into a dark wooden shaft about three feet square. The walls bore insets so a man could climb down to free a stuck bale.

"Follow me," Mueller said, descending into the shaft. I watched him go down about his height, then disappear into the darkness. Following him, I saw he'd gone into a blind alley that couldn't be seen from the top. He said "Stand right past the shaft. Don't move." With that, a set of planks identical to the walls of the lift slid past him. When they opened again, he was gone. A voice said "Do the same." I did. The wall closed over and I was inside a compartment with Mueller. A moment passed and then the box descended—perhaps ten feet, maybe more. In any event, when the box opened again we were inside a room about half the size of the barn, whose walls were lined with cubicles, like the nooks in a warehouse. Mueller took me past them; inside each sat a person, facing away, wearing earphones, in front of a radio set.

"So here we have the reason I want you to get out of here as fast as possible, Captain. For some perverse reason you managed to land yourself atop my little operation. Those people are listening to German signals traffic, and of course, to yours as well."

I was dumbfounded. "You put this all within five miles of the German front?"

"It wasn't the front until your army pushed to the Rhine. We used to be far to the rear."

"Who are these people?"

"Disloyal Germans; some escaped French slave-workers. The last two cubbyholes contain two of your downed airmen—a pair of gunners. We had them 'killed' by patriotic Germans not far from here and buried a little ways off. By the way, give me your dog tags. We're going to have to bury you, too. We put the tags on the cross."

"I imagine my squadron thinks I'm dead."

"Actually, no. We got word to them that you are very much alive."

"Can I talk to the two Air Corps guys?"

"Upstairs. They should be in the barn now."

We found them in the barn, helping to shove my airplane between the wide-spread doors. With a forty-foot wingspan, it had to go in on an angle. One of them called out "You ain't no cripple. Get over here and push."

I did, but said "Fighter pilots are too good for manual labor." This produced a laugh and several curses. When the P-47 was settled, a man introduced himself to me as Sergeant Culvain; the other being Sergeant Ordman. Culvain said "I think we got enough oil to fill your tank if the plugs hold."

"What plugs?"

"The one's we're gonna make. I'm gonna pack shaved lead into the pockets. That should hold you for a few minutes."

"You really expect me to fly out of here in this thing, down that road?"

"Well, if you don't, you can drive it to France. You're five miles from the Rhine now. Only thing is, the Germans are thick along the last stretch."

I turned to Mueller. "When's this circus supposed to start?"

He said "The Germans will come snooping around in a day or so. We can't have you compromise our position. You'll have to leave soon. We're planning it all now."

"Planning what?"

He said "Okay. Every evening at sunset the Americans set up a barrage of the German positions along the river. The Germans, of course, reply. Tonight your people are going to start shooting a little early. They will fire for three minutes and quit. The Germans will begin firing right after this. Since they are close, it will be all 105mm howitzers and some heavy machine guns. The Germans are short on ammunition. They will shoot five rounds—no more. This will take just about one minute. Your job is to get that plane to about a mile of the Rhine just when they begin firing."

"That way there will be too much noise and commotion to see me."

"Yes. And their machine gunners will be targeted on zones of fire along the opposite bank."

"Why is the barrage early?"

"We asked for it. You'll need a bit of daylight to see where you're going. Captain, you're going to have to fly about fifty feet above the ground. There's no cover. It's all farmland. Any higher and they'd see you miles away."

I spent the afternoon in the loft, eating cheese and drinking a very dry German wine. The sun cut interminably downward through the cloudless sky, until it was about two hands above the horizon. Mueller appeared. He said "Come on down and we'll see what we've got."

The plane didn't look any different, except it had been turned toward the barn doors. Sergeant Culvain wiped his hands on a rag and said "She looks good. Fixed the radio. Shock broke the crystals loose. Works fine now. Give her a kick."

I climbed up and did the pre-flight to calm myself down. When I hit the motor, she fired up, threw a bit of smoke, and settled into an asthmatic rendering of the usual roar. It would run; whether it would fly was something else altogether.

Mueller said "We're going to pull her to the road. Take my bicycle down and wait for us."

I watched my machine being hiked along behind the mule team. Minus her cowling she looked like a Great War veteran, but why not? I was about to try an Eddie Rickenbacker takeoff from a dirt field: all of which made about as much sense as anything else on that day.

At the roadway my plane made a dip to the right that nearly buried a wingtip in turnips. They got her straightened out, the mules pulled their traces away, and I was left alone with Mueller and his bicycle. He said "All good. She's still hot and will crank up fast. Your sergeant says to ignore the manifold pressure and the RPM readings. Check your watch. You have five-and-a-half minutes to go. There's two kilometers of flat road ahead of you. If that's not enough you wouldn't be able to make it home anyhow. Your radio is set to our frequency. We'll give the signal."

With that he shook my hand and added "Did you ever carry mail?" I frowned. "No? Well, here's your first opportunity. Send these off the first chance you get." With that he handed me a packet tied with a bit of yarn, then turned away, pedaling back up the dirt path to the place he called home.

The cockpit looked the same except that there was a scrap of paper tied to my gunsight. An oily scrawl on it read 'She will get power. Don't adjust turbo. Fly it off the ground but take the wheels up quick. Drink a beer for me."

I went through the list: *Gas selector on Main; trim tabs in Takeoff position; flaps up*. I didn't have to worry about the cowl flaps being open because there weren't any. I locked the tail wheel. Just then the barrage began—distant thunder capped by muffled blasts. It grew to a crescendo as the gunners tried to get off their rounds in the time window. My plane cranked like a champ and almost sounded normal. After a little while the radio crackled "Give a wave if you roger." I waved. The voice added "Do not transmit. Keep your button up. Thirty seconds."

I counted down as a pilot does, backward; we hit zero at the same moment and the voice said "Good flying." That was all.

I let off the brakes, pushed the throttle with a sweated hand and watched the country start to move. You can't see ahead of you in a P-47 until she starts to fly. I knew that her wheels had very little road to the sides; otherwise I had only the rows of green to keep me on line. As soon as we got rolling she started to shimmy and I had to fly her on the ground. I couldn't look at the airspeed indicator. If she didn't hit the right number there was nothing I could do. It seemed like most of Germany went past before she nudged up into the sky—or at least the portion that I'd be occupying.

It's instinctive for a pilot to get as much altitude as possible after take-off. Resisting that was murder. I took her to about a hundred feet and then slowly down to treetop level. At the top of the hump I saw the arcs of the shells coming from France, and a line of flashes where they hit the German lines this side of the river.

Very suddenly, a jet of black fluid flew backward toward me, billowing into vapor as it passed the canopy. Just as quickly it burst into flame, an angry orange sign that my engine hadn't been bandaged tight enough. I didn't need the gauges to tell me that I was losing power; she dipped hard and I was only able to keep her aloft by fighting the stick. At low speed a plane maneuvers poorly—this one decided to veer right, taking me over a farm field. I couldn't cut her hard without losing altitude, so I just kept going in that direction, losing the road and my path to the river.

For a minute or so my plane tried to mow down the fodder of the Rhineland as I tried just as hard to keep her away. Then, suddenly as it began, the fire died out. I gave her some rudder to return to the road, and found it—or one like it. I knew I was headed southwest—everyone in that direction spoke French. The problem was, I ran into a lot of people who didn't.

The plan fell apart. The Germans were not distracted. To my horror, their tracers turned away from the river, and sideways, at me. The brand-new evening exploded with white-hot hornets, all headed my way. The road made a dog-leg, and I saw the tracers explode in endless ranks before me, like a thousand Roman candles. The flyer's safety net is altitude, which gives maneuvering room, which is life itself. I had none of that, but I had nothing to lose. If I was going to die, I was going to die like a pilot. It was time to get flying.

I gave the engine her head and she gave me elevation. Now I could roll right or left. The tracers now cut curves and loops as they tried to catch me. I felt a few whacks hit the fuselage but saw nothing tear off behind. I decided to give them something to write home about. I hit the toggle to arm the rockets and rose to a thousand feet. From there I could see the arrangement of the guns, and even their crews. I put the dot on a large pack and let go a double shot. The motors blazed out from under my wings, beating me to the spot by a good five seconds. There was an ugly flash and a spray of debris, but by then I had turned away.

I fired another pair at a set of flashes, ruining a battery, and then another and another until my pylons were empty. The Rhine was a thick, beckoning ribbon, but I had eight machine guns left and shot them dry before turning to the French side. A few tracers spat up a farewell as I crossed over.

I was three minutes into France when the radio crackled. "Thunderbolt Flight Leader, maintain altitude, come to course 120. Field is marked with white flares."

I put down the gear and laid her on the ground just as if nothing had happened. It wasn't my home runway, but it wasn't a hayfield in Germany, and it would do.

The crew chief saw the smoking engine in the lights of his jeep, laughed and said "This is why we can't have nice things." Then he handed me a bottle of something rich, dark, and hot. I drank a good swig and then went inside for the briefing.

The Last Doctor   Michael McGrorty

To this day I can't tell you exactly where, except that it was Italy, winter of 1944. By that time the Germans decided that they wanted nothing more of the country than to use it to bleed us white, and they did a good job. I was stationed with a hospital unit, full surgical staff. We kept close enough to the front lines so casualties would arrive with enough life in them that we could do something. Any closer in, you'd get blown up; any further and you'd be running a morgue by the time the trucks got in. If you need to know, draw a line three miles back of the front; find the largest intact structure, and that's where we'd be.

We'd arrive in the dead of night, having been dragged bag and baggage from the previous encampment, rising to a new and yet identical landscape of blasted trees, cratered roads, and the smoking ruins of whatever the Germans had been holed up in prior. After that it was a thick torrent of red until the front line shifted northward, with us close behind.

I never wanted to be a doctor. I had no settled idea, but I blurted out that I wanted to be a *song writer* to my father when I was fifteen, right after he found out that I'd nearly failed chemistry. He'd invited me to lunch on a weekday—never a good sign—and I somehow imagined that the blow would be lessened if I were to show him initiative toward another field of endeavor. We were in the Café Rouge at the old Detroit Statler, and the old man had just come from a morning of rounds in his clinic. He heard my announcement, placed his hand flat upon the linen tablecloth and pronounced, "Joseph, no son of mine is going to fool around with that sort of junk. You are going to do two things: begin tutoring in chemistry, and after that, anything else required for you to attend medical school and hopefully, become a credit to your family and upbringing."

To that point I had not been working terribly hard in bringing credit to either. One reason was that my older brother Louis never required tutoring in chemistry, or anything else, and was already an established orthopedist in Manhattan. It seemed to me that the family gods had been sufficiently propitiated thereby, and after all, Louis had set a rather high bar. But I knew better than to differ with my father on such matters, and soon returned to virtue's path.

Not that there weren't detours. Most of these came in the form of after-hours joints scattered around the periphery of my undergraduate institution, and also, around the medical college I managed to attend. In the former I distinguished myself principally as a composer of late-period ragtime; in the latter, as an aficionado of jazz as played in Negro bars, clubs, and theaters. I would not have been in med school but for my father's influence on the board of the second-level school that accepted me. This school was situated in the Paradise Valley of Detroit, blissfully close to the best of the jazz clubs, which meant I could tumble out of, say, the Three Sixes at dawn, catch a couple hours of sleep, and then play doctor until another evening's smoky revel.

I was always on the verge of being tossed out; in fact, I probably would have preferred being kicked to the pavement but for the fact that the draft had begun and my deferment depended upon remaining in school. Thus I stayed, and they let me, but everything changed one Sunday morning in December. All of a sudden they were in a rush to get us graduated: classes were compressed and summer break eliminated. More important, they trained all of us in surgical technique— a heavy hint at what lay ahead. I graduated nine months early and was immediately drafted in the Army Medical Corps.

My first assignment was to an army clinic in England. It was a comfortable spot along the train line to London, and I managed to learn a bit of doctoring between visits to English jazz shrines. We were barracked in a nice set of flats and the war seemed to be on another planet. Our battle casualties were few compared to the number of accident and illness cases; most of these were simply recuperating from earlier surgeries. At about that point the army invaded North Africa, which had the effect of increasing our patient load, and then, to my intense disappointment, requiring my departure to a hospital ship headed for the Mediterranean. With that point my war began.

The army put together pretty good surgical units, composed of people who had done that work in civilian life. There were no amateurs wielding scalpels on that ship—at least not at first. But beginning with Kasserine in '43, the inflow of patients got so heavy that I started to move up the ladder from minor wounds to assisting serious cases. With that the pattern was set for the rest of the war: days of travel or torpor and then an avalanche of ravaged bodies, sometimes for hours, too often for days on end. The only difference between us and the Civil War was sanitation and the success rate. Otherwise it was the same gory tale.

Sicily was invaded in July, and taken in August. The live casualty rate was about 200 a day. I remember Sicily because it was where I did my first bowel resection. I was standing in the usual pool of blood, about to hand an instrument to our chief surgeon when he said "Joe, knock those ends together. Connell suture, clean up and close." It went just like the book and the patient lived.

The first patient I lost was a boy from Altoona, a loader on a 155mm gun who was doing his job when some German spotter found the range and sent over a reply that killed the rest of the crew. We used evacuation tags that showed a front and back view so medics could just sketch out the wounds. This kid's picture looked like the mouse in a Tom and Jerry cartoon. For all that he seemed fairly stable. Two of us started to work on the worst of it, but his abdomen was a mess of perforations and his lungs were barely holding air. The Senior came over and said, "That's all for this one. Administer a half and come to Station Two." I was stunned. The boy's tag showed that he'd already got morphine in the field, and some on arrival. Any more could arrest his respiration. Besides, I thought he could be saved, for no other reason than that I thought that they all should be saved if they came in breathing. This guy was actually talking, which was how I knew his home town. I got yanked off to help with a crushed chest, but my mind never left the artilleryman. They didn't have to tell me he died; I knew when I left he was done.

After the cases cleared our tent, the Senior led me by the arm to the supply shed, handed me a canteen cup of actual bourbon, and said "Listen Joe. They die. We just see the ones that live long enough to get here. That guy had too many holes. There isn't enough plasma in Italy for that sort of thing. Today you worked with me on—what—two dozen men? Saved all of them except for one kid. Drink your booze and hit the hay."

The script never changed: we crept behind the advance, with the Germans holding hard or counter-attacking all the way. When we arrived in a new spot it was because a big push was about to begin. As soon as we set up, our artillery would blast overhead; the next day would come the attack, and that evening, the casualties. This would go on for a few days or weeks, until the ground was taken. We'd spend a day or so clearing out patients, and then it was on to the next attack and the next flood of torn bodies.

At one point on the road to Rome, the company was located in a little school building outside a flattened village near the meeting of two very old, cobbly roads. We'd taken in five days and nights of wounded and were about to head north again. Most of the unit left the night before; I was sitting in the morning sunlight, writing a letter to my brother, when a jeep came bouncing up the road from the foothills to the west. The driver was a black sergeant—which was unusual in two ways: black men seldom made sergeant in the army, and they were almost never seen in our theater. The man climbed off and made straightaway for the remaining tents, shouting "Who's in charge here?" Somebody must have told him I was, and he made for me like a bayonet thrust.

"You the doctor?"

"The last one," I answered.

"Get in the jeep."

I stole a sidelong glance at the distant surgical tent, which was being taken down by a pair of disinterested privates. The visitor bent toward me.

"Get in that jeep, Lieutenant. I don't want to have to shoot you."

The sergeant was equipped with both a carbine and a .45 pistol, and, having repaired many bullet wounds, I did not wish to test his resolve. I sat in the jeep and said "You got a field kit?" He nodded and hit the gas. We were on our way to somewhere.

The Italians were the first great road builders, but you couldn't tell it by the path we took. In fact, apart from the largest highways, the Italian roads were simply improvements on Roman pathways—and very little improved, at that. Our direction was roughly west, into the foothills. As we bounced along I said to him "I didn't think they had action this way. How many you got?"

"Four or five."

"What happened?"

"Mine. Was supposed to be cleared but we hit a big one. More'n one."

"Why did you get me? You could have brought him down. You're in a transport company."

"It was our last two trucks."

"No infantry patrols?"

My driver turned sideways. "How long you been in this army? White infantry don't transport Negro soldiers. We there two hours and not a one of them stop."

I might have formed an image of the sergeant trying to wave down a passing infantry vehicle, but instead my mind began clicking off the time since the explosion.

"How long did it take you to get to me?"

"'Bout an hour."

That was bad news. We'd lost too much time. "You dress those wounds?"

"Yeah."

That didn't relieve me. I'd seen dressings by ordinary soldiers. You did not want to get bandaged by your regular G.I. I said nothing for a spell and then asked "Where you from?"

"Detroit."

"Where?"

"Brush Street. You?"

"Detroit. Indian Village." With that it was understood that we were raised three miles and a universe apart. My father's house was a granite pile built in a neighborhood intended for wealthy people. The sergeant's home, whatever it was, lay in a ghetto; not exactly a slum, but teetering on the edge. Whatever his people did, they did at the grace and allowance of whites. If they worked at an auto plant, they were in the foundry, or in whatever paid the least and had the most obnoxious work. If they tried to rise, they were put down. In 1942, Packard Motor advanced three black men to the assembly line. In response, 25,000 white workers walked off the job. It was like that. And when blacks were drafted, nearly all were put in Engineering or Transportation, which meant digging ditches or driving trucks. Even combat was too good for Negroes.

I said "Your people new or been here?"

"Been since before I was born. They live in a house—lived in one—'till last June. You know, when the riots came. They been back with my uncle in Memphis since then."

What he meant was that his folks were scared out of town when white rioters smashed through the black sections of Detroit, beating and terrorizing residents.

"What happened to the house?"

"It's there. My brother's in it. He's holding it for me. I'm not gonna leave. They were pissed off that we got places in the Sojourner Housing and came unglued. That's tough. We're gonna have lots of places after the war. They better get used to it."

"You do any damage?"

He laughed and said "Oh, I got my licks in."

"By the way," I said, "What's your name?"

"Paul Orlean." I told him mine and we shook hands.

"Well Mr. Orlean, what were you doing when the draft got you?"

"I was a bartender at Ollie's."

"If you were, it wasn't on weeknights."

"Yeah? And how'd you know?"

"I was there Monday through Thursday."

"Well, I was there on the hot nights—Friday and Saturday. You get out there a lot?"

"Too much. Nearly failed med school." He laughed and I laughed.

The hills rose to become a set of ridges whose flanks we rode, in and out of the daylight, turning sharply every few thousand yards, wasting space and time with every change in direction. Meanwhile, below us, the main road appeared in the valley below, straight and true, heading northward to Rome and beyond.

My friend said "The Jerries set up their artillery here to cover the highway. Infantry come up and clear them out. We brought ammo and took out wounded. Some of them down to you."

Just below the steering wheel, the fuel gauge needle was leaning as far to the left as possible. I mentioned this to the driver, who said "Nope, it's full. These HQ guys yank out the sender so it looks dry. That way nobody borrows the car."

I said "Where'd you borrow this one?"

His eyes narrowed. "Some Major left it on the road."

"Is that Major alive?"

"Yeah, but he's not happy."

"Think he's going to be happy when you come around?"

"Lieutenant, I'm way past caring about that."

"You don't seem to care too much about how you get your medical help, either."

My friend chuckled. "And if I didn't make you, were you going to come out? What do you people say— 'the only way a Negro gets anything is by stealing.' Well, I just stole you and a jeep."

"Okay," I said, "but aren't you afraid I'm going to turn you in?"

"You have to stand in line behind a Major, Lieutenant."

We couldn't manage more than a fast walk over the rough roadway, which was torn up pretty badly in places, especially where the galleries faced north. We drove around smashed vehicles, some so badly twisted I couldn't tell which side they'd belonged to.

For some reason the Sergeant said "Don't suppose you ever got around to the Pie Cart, down the street from Orchestra Hall?

"Once or twice. Kinda small there."

"Yeah. Just the piano and the bar. I used to bartend there weeknights."

"I remember they had this house guy, Perris Kingly. Genius at stride playing. Used to do this boogie rhythm with the left hand—"

"—and stride melody with the right. Yeah, you know him. He'd watch the hired player all night and then shoot him down, maybe one, two in the morning."

We reached a bend in the road that overlooked the valley below. Above the far horizon, a chevron of B-24s cut their way through a bright blue sky. We turned again toward the hills, into another hairpin, and then another straight.

"How much longer," I asked.

"Just a bit. It levels out right before."

We cut a few more angles against the hillsides, and then the front wheels dropped even with the rear. All at once we were on a plateau where the road curved in the cove of a large stone outcrop. Just off the path lay a pair of six-wheeled trucks, about ten yards apart. Both rested on their driver sides; neither had front wheels. Another truck stood unmarked nearby. The air smelled of explosives and gasoline.

I said to the sergeant "What's in those trucks?"

He said "Don't bother. Just spaghetti."

He pulled over and I went to investigate. I climbed atop the passenger door of the first. Inside was a man, very much mangled, who had been blasted into the roof of the cab. The second truck held two men—at first it looked like one, but then I counted the legs—there were three of them, amidst a wet litter of clothing, bone, and muscle. He was right. Nothing but spaghetti—and cold.

"Where are the others?"

The sergeant "One near the road, another in this truck."

I found a man lying along the road, covered by a tent half, his face no longer black but gray, the color all races share in death. He was warm enough to have died within the hour. I felt his chest. There were broken ribs and a shattered sternum.

I said "This one, he was thrown from the second truck. He bled from the nose and then went quiet?"

"Yeah," said the sergeant.

"Why didn't you bring him down in the jeep?"

"I walked down the road for about a mile before I found the jeep. After that I just kept going."

"You couldn't use this other truck?"

He said nothing, but led me over to the rear of that vehicle. Inside was a jumble of wooden ammo cases. It looked like somebody tried to move the smaller ones. When my eyes adjusted to the darkness inside I saw a pair of legs extending from beneath a very large and obviously heavy metal cube that met them on an angle, pinning a man to the bed of the truck.

I crawled into the bed and felt one of the ankles. It was cold. A voice cracked out from the darkness. "Sarge? That you?"

I said "No, it's a doctor." I scrambled atop the fallen boxes and discovered to my horror that the voice came from the man whose legs were crushed beneath the huge metal box. He was alive—partly.

I backed out quickly and said to the sergeant, "How'd he get there?"

"He was riding in back when the other two hit the mines. Killed the motor, threw all the cargo around and he fell under it. That box is eight hundred pounds of lifting hardware."

I felt my heart pounding like a hammer and managed to say "Christ, what do you expect me to do?"

The sergeant grabbed my right arm near the shoulder and said "You got to save him. That's Perris Kingly."

I said his name as if hearing it again would give me something I could use. Out there, in the middle of practical nowhere, with nothing but the first-aid kit that came with every truck issued to the army, I was supposed to save a man who'd lain hours under a metal box, legs already gone to the next world.

In medical school they taught us to talk our way through procedures—say the steps to ourselves and then follow through. But they never taught us anything about men crushed in six-wheeled trucks. We did our work in a sanitized white cocoon. I felt helpless and afraid: helpless because every important tool I needed was miles distant, and afraid because I could lose this man, the only patient I had ever known in the least before meeting him unconscious on the operating table. And then there was the sergeant. I couldn't get my mind to deal with that at all.

First there was a patient to attend. I said to myself 'obtain vital signs; determine injury and course of action.'

I told the sergeant "You pull off the canvas for some light." I climbed inside and sat atop a box near the man's head. I said "Can you feel your heart in your chest?" He nodded. I added "Count it for me." He sounded off ten beats as the second hand swept the face of my watch. Pulse 90—not bad. And he could speak, strongly. I went on: "Dumbest question on earth: where does it hurt?" He answered, "Nowheres." I said "Raise your arms." He raised them, quickly and strongly.

I made my way carefully over the jumble of boxes to the rear of the truck. In the light I could see my patient's legs had been put in a vice, with the sharp right angle of the steel box pressing through flesh and bone, leaving about two fingers of clearance between the box and the truck floor. I pulled a pencil from my jacket and poked hard at the thigh. There was no response.

From outside the truck, the sergeant barked "What's going on?"

I left the truck and led the sergeant out of hearing range of my patient. I said, "Okay. He's alive enough on top. His legs are gone."

"But his legs are right there, and he's talking. You heard him talk!"

"I heard him talk. He talks just fine. Problem is, he's been under that box—what, three hours now? The legs are dead. If I could get him into surgery right now, this instant, we could maybe save his life. But the moment he gets free of that box, the dead blood in his legs is going to mix with the rest, and he's going to pass into shock. He won't last half an hour."

The sergeant growled "He isn't going to make it under that box, Lieutenant. Come on, we're going to get him out and down the road to the hospital."

We pushed the other boxes far enough away to make a clearance for the metal cube. The sergeant took two hoist bars from the blown-up trucks and put them where he could get some leverage. He said "I'm gonna raise this and you're gonna put a cartridge case under it." With that he leaned all his weight on the left bar, and I kicked a box of .50 caliber rounds underneath. We did it again on the right side, and I saw light above my patient's thighs. Another two lifts, another two boxes, and he was clear enough to move. I pulled as gently as I could on his boots until he slid back toward the tail.

The two of us turned him sideways. As I did I felt his legs flex where the angle of the box had met them. There was no bone there; no living nerve or flesh beyond. But there was life remaining. I said to my patient, "My name is Joseph. And you are?"

"Perris Kingly. Formerly of Detroit, Michigan."

I cracked a most unprofessional grin and said "You have the best pair of hands in Detroit, Mr. Kingly. God bless you."

I watched the pulse in his neck and counted. Two per second; not good. His pupils were enlarged, perhaps from the sunlight, perhaps not. I said to the sergeant "Right now, if we put a tourniquet on those legs, he may live."

The sergeant replied "Nothing doing. He don't want to live without any legs and you aren't going to do that as long as I can stop you."

"All right," I said, "Let's get him in the jeep." We stacked boxes so Kingly could lie flat, his head forward, nearly at the front panel. The sergeant secured him with blankets, I sat behind our driver, and we began our descent.

It went faster, or perhaps only seemed to. The main highway flashed into view and vanished, over and again as we came closer to the valley floor. Every few moments I reached beneath the blankets to grasp my patient's right hand—the one that would wander ever go gently over the keys, then pierce the smoky air of the Pie Cart with cascades of perilous notes over the mad funereal pounding of the left. That hand grew colder by the minute, its pulse gone from march-time to a weak staccato.

I said to him "What did you play that New Year's when Teddy Wilson came around?"

His eyes opened wide, and he rasped "I did 'Lady be Good.' Should have seen his face."

I said "I did. You got a lot of sound from that old upright." I think he smiled.

We reached a place where three short bends lay below us, a sinuous reach like a whiplash uncoiled, its handle touching the main roadway. In the near distance lay the remnant of our hospital, and beyond, the paved highway to Rome.

I reached for the hand again, but the pulse that had driven it was gone.

There would be no more music, no more smoky joints in Paradise Valley or anywhere else this side of the curtain. I stole a glance at the rearview mirror on the windshield and met the sergeant's eyes. He stopped the jeep, yanking the brake handle so hard it sounded like a machine gun firing. He bent over the dead man with a look of terrible defeat, pressed his palms to the blankets and wept like a child.

There was no place for me among them after that; there had been little enough before. I left the sergeant with his grief, walking the last few yards alone. As I reached the last turn, the flight of B-24s passed back toward the south, one plane missing from its chevron.

The Farm Girl   Michael McGrorty

O n an evening in late August, 1942, a young woman stood waiting in the yard of a small cottage twenty miles east of London, face turned against a spattering summer rain. After a few minutes a sedan approached; it stopped and a man exited. He opened the rear passenger door and the woman entered. The car rolled away slowly, its headlights only slits, as if the vehicle were squinting to find the roadway in the dark.

A few miles on, the car passed through the guarded gate of a military base, then continued to a long stretch of new concrete at whose end sat a twin-engined bomber, props turning slowly, squat on its haunches like a dog waiting for its master.

The car let off its passenger a short walk away, whereupon the woman strode to the aircraft and underneath, scarcely bending her head to pass under a wing. An officer appeared, helped her into the fuselage, and latched the door behind. With that the plane spun on its wheels and began a slow roll to the end of the runway.

Inside the aircraft, the woman found a shoulder bag and a flying suit, which she donned as if that were quite an ordinary thing. By the time she was dressed, the plane was speeding down the runway into the wind. Once aloft, a crewman handed her an envelope whose contents she read carefully.

The plane headed southeast, toward an invisible dot over the English Channel. Reaching that place, it turned inland, picked up speed, and crossed over the soil of France. Moments later the crewman appeared in the passageway, slid open the fuselage door and said "Now." The woman, already kneeling at the doorway, tumbled forward into the sky.

There was no rain where she landed, and the farm field was blessedly soft. She tumbled a short way, rose and yanked in the parachute, then looked to the stars. She found Polaris and walked toward a dark jagged place on the horizon that meant a piece of woodland. She found an old stone wall and beyond it, a grove of trees. At that place the ground sloped slightly upward and the earth was stony. This would be where a farmer unloaded rocks levered from his fields. A place nobody would think to go, day or night. She lay against the far side of the stone wall and fell asleep.

Before the first light she buried the flight suit and parachute, dressing herself as if she were a French farm girl—not a difficult thing for she had been for years. At last she pulled on a pair of leather boots, much worn and much repaired, pinned a straw hat to her hair, and began to walk in the direction of a smoking chimney which might have been a half mile away.

There was a road, if not laid by the Romans then improved by them: cobbled, but with curb blocks to keep the edge and line; this went straight to the house with the chimney, as it should. The house was no larger than it had to be in the time of Napoleon. There was a chicken coop built on the base of a dovecote when doves lost favor to chickens. It remained round and reassuring. There was a dog, which met her at the roadside with more curiosity than repulse. It gave the mandatory bark, which brought a farm woman's face to the kitchen window, and then to the side door, whence she emerged, wiping her hands on her apron, face a wordless inquiry.

The two met in the garden next to the road. The farm woman said "Where are you bound?" The younger replied "To Rennes for the market." The other said "Come inside. Rest your feet."

The woman brought cider, fresh and full of the taste of fall apples. She asked "What do you seek in Rennes?"

The younger one said "Oh, cheese and bread. And needles."

"Needles are very dear now."

"I can pay."

"You have the old money?"

The young woman said "Yes," and produced a packet of franc notes. The farm woman found her spectacles. She looked the bills over. They were of different denominations but were arranged so that the last digits of the serial numbers were consecutive.

The other said "Indeed, this is the old money. Wait, I'll get you something for your journey."

She went to another room, returning with her husband, who said "Here is a small cart for you. It is a good distance to the station. You should arrive before the noon train. Take this road north. There are no checkpoints."

The cart was like a folding pram. Inside were several small cheeses in their wax; two squat loaves of crusty bread, and a pair of large brown sausages wrapped in oily paper.

The sky was pale blue and the farm fields bright with summer green. She pushed the cart along, waving to the field workers, who moved slowly, as people do when they must work for the whole of the day. They called to her 'Girl, where are you bound?' She replied "Paris, to see the king."

She came to a place where railroad tracks crossed the graveled farm roadway. It was getting along in the day and she chose to follow the rails rather than the longer path of the road. She folded up the cart, tied its bag to her back and started down the line of fence which marked the boundary of the railroad line.

The cart was heavy, but not too heavy for a farm girl. She might be only forty kilograms, but she had once carried a newborn calf three kilometers from a sodden field to her father's barn. If anything, she became stronger after the men were taken away, because she had to be.

The sun rose higher and the day warmed. Sometimes she stumbled on the coarse rocks of the railway path. The cart bit into her shoulders. She was about to rest when she saw the peak of the station roof ahead. She set down the cart, arranged its contents, and pushed until the platform came into sight.

The ticket-taker asked "Where are you bound?" She answered "I am going to Rennes." He replied "See the station master." This she knew would be a German railroad officer, who might require a bribe, and who would certainly want to see her papers.

It was in fact an unpleasant, oily German with a crooked mouth who asked her "Why are you going to Rennes?"

"For the market."

"To buy or sell?"

"Both. I am a seamstress. I want needles."

The man shifted in his seat before saying "I think you're going there to steal. Show me your money."

The young woman produced her bills; the German inspected them minutely and said "Is that cheese I see?"

"Yes, but I can't share it."

The officer frowned with half his mouth and said "All right then girl— go on. The train arrives soon. Last car, if you please."

He stamped her papers and spun his chair toward the window.

Outside, a mother with two small children waited for the train. It arrived at quarter to twelve, puffing along slowly as if the tracks were too hot to touch. There were six cars: five packed with German infantry, dozing in their seats; ahead of that the coal car and engine; at the very rear, where the cinders would land, a common car for the French. There would be no Frenchmen except the lady, her children, and the traveling woman.

They took their seats as the station clock's hands worked their way upward. At eight minutes to noon, the young woman said to the mother "There is no washroom in this car. It's a long way to the next stop. Perhaps you should take them into the station. Come on, I'll help you."

The German officer and clerk were gone. The key hung where it ought to be; the lady and her two children went into the washroom. As soon as the door closed, the young woman locked the door, tossed the key into the corner, and left. Back in the rail car she removed a small knife from her bag, and cut the skin on one of the long sausages, removing an oblong, black shard, shiny like a piece of anthracite. She left the car again, strolling casually along the line of the cars until reaching the locomotive, whose engineer she found leaning over his dials and gauges. With a deft movement she flipped the black shard into the scuttle of waiting coal, then returned back to the last car of the train.

At noon the engineer levered the train to life. It rattled along the tracks for a few meters, then halted at a water tank. The traveling woman stepped from the rear door of the car, lifted her cart onto her back, and began walking eastward. She found the fence line of a farm and went along this for a while; then north; then west again. When her legs became tired, she stopped to eat, breaking one of the loaves for her meal.

A good distance away, beyond of sight and hearing, the locomotive's engineer pulled the scuttle along its pair of grooves toward the firebox, then tipped the tub into the chute and closed the iron door. He had no more than turned away when the body of the locomotive split along its welded seams, throwing fire and steam into the sunshine. The undercarriage raced along dumbly until its trucks went separate ways, which sent the cars of German infantry snaking off the tracks, careening left and right down the embankment, tumbling over and over, windows shattering, metal warping, human cargo cut, crushed, and then burned when the firebox coals fell back upon the wood of the ruined cars.

After her meal the traveler resumed her journey, rolling her cart when she could, carrying it when she must. Near to dusk she came to a small village. She inquired as to lodgings and was told to find the widow Fleming, who happened to reside in a little stone house, tidy and neat, somewhat removed from the others. She found the widow in her garden, cutting greens for supper.

The traveler said "Good evening, Madame. I would like to inquire about lodging for one night."

The widow, none too pleased, replied "Go away. I have no room for strangers."

The stranger replied "All right. I will sleep in your field. Is there water?"

The widow said "There is a pump ten paces to the west. Go now, before it's too dark to see."

The pump was old and its seals leaky. She managed to draw up a pail of water; washed her face, hands and feet, then raked up a pile of leaves to make a bed beneath a gnarled apple tree. She drew her shawl about her shoulders and fell asleep quickly, as one does after a day of walking.

In the house, the widow chopped her garden greens, added a sliced potato, and a small chicken to a simmering pot of broth. The fire of the stove lit the tiny kitchen in faint flashes through slats in its iron firebox. The widow stirred her soup, poured herself a cup of lemon grass tea and settled into a chair near the fire.

Outside, beneath the apple boughs, the traveler began to dream. She saw herself sitting in the open door of an aircraft, then suddenly falling away toward the ground far below. A parachute opened; she floated gently downward to a place along the edge of a stream, a farmstead bordered by lines of hedge enclosing thick, dark-green grass. She hung in space for a time, seeing all this, and then began to sink as if by will toward the garden of the brick house and its timber barns. It was a beautiful summer day: cattle lowed in the fields; ducks squabbled in the little pond; a woman tied pea vines to canes in rich garden soil.

But as she came closer, the sunshine faded, though the sky was cloudless. Now the roof of the brick house was gone; the barns smashed to kindling; the animals fled; the garden in disarray. When her feet reached the ground, she shrugged off the parachute and ran through the doorway of the house, and saw its wrecked furniture, broken tiles and fractured walls beneath the sky. And there, on the littered floor, a bloody shirt that had been her father's.

She ran, partly through the air, rounding the ruined barns, calling out her mother's name, but there was no answer. At last she found her, sitting in the garden, filthy and torn, eyes vacant. She said "Mother, what has become of us?" The mother's face shivered to life and she said "The Germans did this because you joined the resistance."

In her sleep the young woman stiffened. The widow stood above her in the darkness, laid a blanket over her sleeping form, and returned to her cottage.

Dawn found the traveler moving to the north-west, rolling or carrying her cart depending on the path. When she saw a steeple, she avoided it; when she came upon a hamlet, she skirted its edge; where there were woods, she passed along their shaded margins, just inside the line of trees, beyond sight of the fields. By afternoon she was walking beside an endless course of sunflowers, each head turned to face the sun in its journey. She kept to the path alongside that field, looking for a sign.

Nearly at noon—not by the clock but the sun—she noticed a fragment of sunlight reflecting from the loft of a barn in the distance. The light flared, then flared again: three short flashes and a longer one. Upon that she described a circle with her arm, then disappeared into the stalks of the sunflowers.

A farmer came along, hoe over one shoulder, whistling. The traveler emerged, head and shoulders sprinkled with bright yellow pollen. The man said "Where are you bound, flower-girl?"

"To the market in Rennes."

"And why?"

"I am a seamstress. I want needles."

"Ah," the man replied. "So many go there in this season. Come with me."

He led her along the edge of the field and down a lane to the barn she had seen. Its large doors were open; inside was an older man, drinking wine at a table. He looked up and said "What is in your bundle, girl?"

"Cheese and sausage for the market."

He extended a hand. "Let me have a look." She replied "Leave it for now. I can show you tonight."

"No.," he said. "Everything has come closer now. We have to leave for another place. Before sunset."

"All right," she said. "I will show you. Is there a spade?"

The man brought her a garden trowel. "Is this right?"

"Good enough. First, you cut a round hole about the length of your foot. Make it about half as much deep, with a solid bottom." She traced out a circle in the dirt of the barn, then cut it deeper with the trowel point until it was about a hand-span in depth.

"Now, take your package out. You have only one chance to do this right. Place the carton into the hole. Fill the sides with soil—like this. Now, tamp the soil down with the flat of the spade."

The men watched carefully but without expression. The farmer said "Where is the detonator?"

"There is none. That was the problem with the others. The detonators broke off. Watch me. You peel back the label on the top—not the wax board, just the paper. Inside the label is a thin wire. When you tear it, the wire breaks and the box is ready. After that, you bury the thing in dirt. But by God, don't step on it. If you do, the next step on top will set it off."

The wine drinker said "How many for us?"

"Four."

"But we need more."

The young woman set her face and said "They need them as much down the road as here."

There was no argument. Their business being done, she left for the fields with the farmer. He led her down a furrowed cart path that passed a waste tip. From the piles of dirty straw came the smell of fresh blood. The farmer mumbled "Don't mind that. We had to kill a pig."

Half a kilometer beyond, the farmer squatted and drew a diagram in the dust with his finger, saying "Northwest is the road junction—five kilometers. Heavily patrolled. The way around is above, through the woods. After that, the villages, and then the city. Girl, leave us those boxes. It is impossible for you to reach Rennes without being inspected."

She reached for his hand, grasped its hard palm, and said "It will be done."

From his side she began to walk to the northwest, then, when he was out of sight, she turned directly south, making half an hour's distance before turning once again, toward the setting sun. Darkness found her in a field of brush, far from buildings, roads, or people.

She lay down, wrapped in her woolen shawl; not warm, but warm enough, and fell asleep. She tumbled through dreams: of places and times gone forever, mixtures of memories; plans and fears and longings, mingled without order or boundary:

She was walking down the road from her farm to the closest village, wearing her pale-yellow church dress because it was Easter. She carried her shoes, and also a birch wand at whose end she had tied spring flowers with a bit of blue ribbon. Along the way she met others on the same journey. At the village gate they came together, formed two files and continued toward the churchyard, the eldest man at the head, carrying a small statue of the Risen Christ. The village priest waited at the gate, turned its latch, and admitted them.

The service was beautiful and joyous. Daylight shone through the small, bright windows of the stone chapel, throwing sharp shafts of light upon the assembly. Behind them, the choir began a hymn; not in Latin but French. On the shaded side of the aisle, closest to the wall, she was in her favorite place, among the saints and martyrs carved into the stone.

Her eyes wandered along the reliefs, and then to the lowest window, its leaded pane behind a grill of wrought iron. Outside there would be a table, and upon that, a luncheon spread for the parish. But the choir faded to silence in the middle of a verse; the shafts of light bent away, emerging on the opposite side, glaring through the glass, throwing the mark of iron upon the pews.

Instead of the priest there was a German officer at the naked altar, waving a rod and shouting in broken French. The assembly was dressed in their work clothes, farmers, wives, children—all as they had been taken from the fields and houses to bear witness. The officer's face and neck were a red glow atop his gray uniform, like a railroad lantern rolling on his shoulders. At last he concluded, with the phrase "Pour chacun de nous dix d'entre vous!" And they were permitted to leave—not by the rear doors, but through the side, into the churchyard, where lay the bodies of the mayor, the priest, the miller, and seven others, laid out on angled planks against the stone wall, their blood in narrow rivulets flowing to pool together.

The first sun shone through rolling clouds: clean, white, like the wool of lambs tumbling across the sky. The ground was damp with dew and the traveler coughed her first waking breaths into the daylight. Her back was stiff and her legs still sore from the day before. She stretched, then searched the ground for a sprig of horehound, which grew in every place the plow did not touch. Finding one, she pulled off three leaves, rolled them between her palms, and placed them in her cheek.

In the near distance was a house, half-timbered as they would all be between there and the coast, for she was in Brittany now, a place where her French would stand out against the Breton accent. Her safeguard was the market in Rennes, where many could be expected to attend, sometimes journeying days, as she had. Even so, she could not risk inspection and so must thread along toward the city through its outskirts, avoiding the obvious routes.

And then there was the problem of the train station at Rennes, southeast of the city. It was a most unsafe place, and yet she must go there, or fail her mission. The Germans had stripped the land around the tracks of concealment; there was only the line of rails, and the sidings, for three kilometers leading to the station. The tracks were blocked by a line of fence and patrolled by soldiers with guard dogs. It was impossible to reach the trains, and yet she must.

Three kilometers of steady walking took her to the margin of the fence, a sinister electrified affair hung with warning placards. She saw others there and followed their path toward the town, but paused at a checkpoint controlling access to a bridge that crossed over the rail lines and the river. She saw that the booth was occupied by single soldier, French, and quite young. She approached and said "I have a delivery for Monsieur Jourdan. Can you have him called?" The soldier, who did not wish to admit that he had no idea who or where Monsieur Jourdan might be, ignored the request, and examined the woman's papers with great gravity before allowing her to proceed.

The bridge was built of iron straps in a riveted lattice pattern, painted dull green, begrimed with ages of locomotive soot. Beneath its curve were electric signals, one for each set of tracks.

She had not planned to cross the bridge but did so because of an opportunity which presented itself—a chance to avoid a great risk by taking a lesser one. As she pushed the cart along the grillwork surface of the bridge walkway, she saw below her lines of open rail cars on sidings, each filled with coal confiscated from the French. The fuel had been stockpiled for the Rennes power station, but was taken to feed the war industries and power plants of Germany. The French were left to subsist on poor, sulfurous coal which hardly produced heat, smoked badly and stank wherever used. This good coal, the stuff bought from England years before, was bound for the Ruhr.

She gazed downward as she walked, watching the grillwork of the walkway line up with spots on the ground; on the empty cars; finally, on the open coal bins. When a square of decking lined up with a coal wagon, she reached into her cart, twisted out a piece of the hard-black stuff which so much resembled coal, and dropped a piece through the grating to fall into the anthracite below. Her heart was a pounding hammer but her face remained calm. To have noticed, a person would have to be watching very closely, and if they were, it didn't matter. All that mattered was that the work was done. In a few moments she had completed that part of her mission; all that remained was to approach Rennes, and wait for the morning.

Beyond the rail lines lay *La Vilaine*, the river which had been turned into a canal after powering windmills for centuries. The railroad had not yet rendered it obsolete, but the Germans had cut off access to the sea, so it had been reduced more or less to a conduit for vegetables between Breton towns. The bargemen of the canal were, as those on any river, fiercely independent. Their proudest claim—sometimes true—was that they had never slept a night on land. They disliked the French authorities and despised the Germans.

The traveler pushed her cart in the direction of the river, which, having been sealed at its ends by the invader, was thought to have been rendered secure. The river made its way through a stone channel with tow-paths to either side; in places where roads met the stream, its channel broadened for the mooring of barges, some owned by families which had held rights to the same spot for a century or more. She pushed along, searching for a barge painted pale blue. She saw none at the first cove; none again at the second, but found one at the third, on whose bow was the name *Muriel*. The ship was masted, though she had likely not unfolded sheets on open water since the war began.

The young woman approached the *Muriel* and called out a name. A man's head appeared in a narrow doorway, wearing a not-particularly-friendly expression. Upon seeing her, he ran his hand over his hair, called out a name to the inside of the boat, and said "Come aboard if you've something to sell, but do not trouble me with trifles."

She stepped onto the deck of the *Muriel* and said "I offer no trifles."

"Then what have you?"

"I have cheese, and the good, old money," she said, producing a packet of bills which she placed on a stool between them. The man sat on the deck and said "Indeed. And what will you buy?"

"I am a seamstress and want needles."

"Needles," the man said loudly, and a boy approached holding one between his finger and thumb. The bargeman flipped through the packet of bills, and chose a two-franc note, which he placed flat on the wooden stool. He then reached into his vest pocket, producing another bill. He arranged these to cover one another and traced two diagonal lines on them with his fingernail, running corner to corner. At their intersection he pushed the needle through the paper, then lifted up both bills, making a sort of pinwheel, which he held up to the sunlight. He rotated the notes against each other until reaching a certain place; whereupon he gazed deliberately into the pattern thus made, which formed letters and words. When the message was memorized, he set the two bills down in small ceramic bowl, lit a match, and burned them to ash.

Glasses were brought out, and a bottle of *Bourgueil* uncorked. The traveler said "How did you save this?"

"I have a cache nearby. I put its labels on cheaper stuff and sell that to the Nazis."

She glanced about for the boy, and not seeing him, said "How old is he now?"

"Twelve. His mother wants him in school, but he won't go."

"Where is his brother?"

"Alan is a guest of the Germans. He started out as a laborer on the Kiel Canal, but now he's running a boat. Gets paid a little. Writes home all the time. The letters of course are intercepted. He tells of his love for Germany. I write back that Hitler is a fine leader. This keeps the Nazis out of our business—except for the wine."

She finished her glass and said "I must be going. How about a bottle of that for a gift?"

"That's the last *Bourgueil*, but I have something better. And you must stay here. It is too dangerous outside."

"Where I am is always too dangerous, which is why I will not stay. Goodbye, my friend, and thanks for the wine."

They shook hands on the tow path and the man whispered "Tomorrow night. Eight o'clock, at the *cidrerie*."

Daylight was dying in the trees along the tow path as she left the boat.

When it was almost too dark to see, she turned into the woods beside the stone path, went a distance into the maze of their trunks, then doubled back, lay down on her shawl, and slept.

She dreamt of a boy who sat behind her in elementary school. She did not like him because he was a boy, and disliked that boys were put in the same classes as girls, though she knew it was because their school was so small there could be no division. They sat according to name, and his followed hers, so she was fated to have this boy seated behind her until the end of their schooling in the district. She was resigned to this but not by any means content, because the boy had the tendency to bother her in various ways. He liked to whisper her name, and to send her notes, and to do other ridiculous and distracting things, which seemed to fall beneath the notice of the *professeur.* The boy's goal seemed to be to make her laugh, which she steadfastly refused to do, until the last year before matriculation, when he sent her an unbidden letter containing a long story about a farm dog, which she read over the All Saints holiday, being afterward convinced of two things: that the boy could make her laugh, and indeed, make her cry.

After elementary school they went separate ways—she to the girl's *college*, and he to the boys' equivalent. These were far apart, which she felt would provide relief from his presence. But it was an emptiness she discovered instead, and a longing for ridiculous notes and jokes that were only two-thirds funny at best. With no voice whispering her name, she became lonely—to the point where she replied to one of his letters, which only managed to find her hands because of a friend who could be trusted to keep secrets. After that they corresponded, often at great length, and met with one another at their parents' homes, maintaining all the decorum called for in that day, though their elders suspected, if they didn't know, that the two were irretrievably lost.

And then, in an ugly stroke, the war came, and defeat, and death, and disorder, and the loss of hope and the future, which no young person can ever lose but will seek to find in whatever remains regardless of cost. The boy trained as a pilot but left for England after the Nazi triumph, remaining to fly missions for the RAF. She followed him, accepting missions of another kind.

She dreamed of that boy, and his lame jokes, and the day when he returned from *college* a head taller than she, deep-voiced and dreadfully handsome, to present her with a promise so absurd that she refused to even consider it. She thought of the promise now, but only in sleep, letting go the words with wakening and the start of another day.

In the morning her cough was gone and the stiffness in her limbs also. She took this for a good portent. Beyond the tow path and the canal, the road was filling with travelers, all of them moving toward Rennes and its *Marché de Lices*—the Saturday market.

To the Germans, the Rennes market was an uncontrolled bazaar wherein a black market might flourish, taxes be evaded, and strangers mingle in dangerous ways. In short, it functioned as it had under every other regime for hundreds of years. But the importance of the Rennes market had always been its position between the productive farmlands of Brittany and the bounty of the sea. Rennes had been the point of departure for many a shipment of goods and grain via *La Vilaine*, and the importation of many things from the outside world through the same artery. With the strangling of canal trade, the German occupiers considered themselves safe from outside harm, which left them to focus upon such harms as might be brought from the interior.

It said much about the German ability to exert control that it had taken her three days and much care to arrive at a spot which had been half a day distant before the war. In addition, they had sown the town with police, soldiers, informers, and agents: watchers and listeners for every sound, act, and utterance—especially on Market Saturday.

The Rennes market took place in the shadow of the *Cathedrale Saint-Pierre*, with sellers scattered about the streets leading to the church. The first challenge would be passing into the city proper. The Germans maintained a checkpoint along the main road. This was easily evaded, but no one could enter the market without the pass issued at its booth.

The young woman moved along slowly with the rest of the travelers, nearly all of them women or old men, from the outskirts to the boundary of the town. Nearing the inspection booth, she shifted the two loaves of bread to the top of her pile of goods, and placed the bottle of wine in plain sight. The inspector, one of the kind of men who relishes such work, insisted that each person turn out his bundle so that the items could be inspected. She complied, removing her wares so they could be viewed. The man took special pleasure in criticizing the travelers' goods; he seemed to have a harsh word for each and every item. Even so, he did not demand that the bearers open their packages.

He approached the young woman and prodded her pile of stacked cheeses with a stick until it toppled. "Ah, the usual country garbage," he sneered. "Your soft cheeses are like mud. A dog would not eat them. But here—" he said, looking at the bottle on the ground— "what is *this* thing? A dry white Bordeaux? You must have stolen it. Let me see—" now he examined the liter bottle carefully.

"My God," he continued, "had you intended to sell this? And for how much?"

"Ten francs," she replied."

"Five and no more," he responded. Before she could refuse, he grabbed the bottle by its neck, threw a bill in her face and strutted down the line to the next person. She looked at the bill—it was one of the practically worthless ones issued by the Nazis. Instead of 'Liberté, égalité, fraternité,' its motto now read 'Travail, famille, patrie.'

A clerk at the booth gave a cursory glance to her papers and pinned a 'market card' to her lapel, indicating she passed inspection. Now there was only a short bit of distance to the open place of the market booths and stalls. But as she rounded the corner which marked the entry to the marketplace, she saw a rope barrier between two poles, and behind that, a pair of dark-uniformed Vichy security policemen. They had seen her at the same moment. If she turned back now it would mean a short pursuit and capture. Instead, she rolled her little cart closer, and made a sharp turn to the left, directly into a covered stone archway where a thick oak door stood. She turned its bronze handle, which opened, admitting her to the aisle of the great Cathedral.

Inside it was cool as stone, with sunlight filtering through the great windows. Tall marble pillars cast their shadows across the aisle. Against a wall, between two sunlit spaces lay a rack of votive candles before a figure of the Virgin. A woman knelt before them; rose, dropped a coin in the box, lit a wick, crossed herself, and departed. She was followed by others, would be all this market day, as buyers took the chance to visit the cathedral from distant places.

The young woman set her cart beside the row of hard wooden chairs and sat, as if waiting for a moment before the Virgin. An old man approached, whispering "Have you any coins? I have only these bills." He presented her with a wad of franc notes bearing the old motto, and muttered "I am going blind. Can you read them?"

Indeed, she could, but she offered the man a handful of coins without taking his money. He said, "Kneel with me, won't you? My knees are not good." They approached the shrine and knelt together. Softly he said, "*Au nom du Pere et du Fils et du Saint-Esprit, Amen.*" And then, "Take your cart to the bench beneath the statue of St. Paul. We will come and get them. This is from Andre."

She replied "Who is Andre?"

"I am Andre, and there is no one else on earth who could know why you are here. Go on. You have only a short while before a funeral."

Having no other choice, she rolled her cart to the bench beneath St. Paul and waited, eyes fixed on her lap, for whatever would come.

An older woman approached, sat without a word upon the narrow bench, and began to pray silently. She placed her coat upon the stone floor to kneel; upon rising, she let the coat fall upon the cart as she arranged her stockings. At that, the younger one thrust one of the boxes into the sleeve of the coat. A moment later the woman departed.

Another woman appeared, said a prayer, and set her coat down on the bench between them. She left with a small parcel in her pocket.

The exchanges continued until the boxes were gone. The ninth visitor muttered "I am the last. Leave by the door right of the altar. The police stay to the other side."

Outside the church, a small group assembled as a rough wooden casket was lifted from the rear of a hearse. Her gaze fell upon a knot of men standing a few yards beyond, whose attitudes indicated a serious duty. They wore the clothes of faraway cities, places, perhaps, beyond even France. She moved a few steps to one side, to see if their eyes would follow her, but there was no notice. At least they did not have her description—yet.

The group of mourners entered the cathedral, leaving the casket on its rolling bier. She strode to the driver's side of the hearse and said to him, "Ten francs if you can take me a kilometer from here. There is enough time before you must return."

The thought of earning ten francs overcame any hesitation he might have had. He said nothing, started the motor and motioned toward the opposite door. When they had begun to travel, she said "Toward Saint-Gregoire, if you please." In a few minutes' time they were at the edge of the city—at first in the area of large houses, then smaller ones; finally, to the place where the green fields began. They came to a place where the road ended against a plank fence. She said "Very good. Thank you," and handed the man three five-franc bills, but he returned one, saying "We bargained for ten."

She rolled her empty cart down the first farm lane leading from the road, and then sidelong onto another, and another, going west and north, west and north, heading for a stand of tall trees upon a hill far from any buildings. Reaching that point she made way almost to the top, pausing every few moments to see if she was followed. The sun tipped toward the horizon. She waited in the shade of the trees, holding up a twig to figure the route to her objective. Not far away, the fields of grain and potatoes gave way to stands of fruit trees, and especially, the hard, tart apples which the French use for *cidre*.

The cathedral bells sounded the hours as the day passed through its life. At five in the evening she began her descent to the fields; at six she was within them; by seven, at the margin of the orchards. She forsook the dirt roads at that point, passing through the fruit trees, seeing the bounty of the countryside heavy on the bough. The apples were a month, perhaps two, from harvest; much would depend upon the time of the first frost. When the day came, they would be shaken down, raked into baskets, and taken in horse-drawn wagons to the press, which was never far from the fields, because nobody would know how to blend apples for *cidre* but a farmer, and because the remains of the pressing—the pomace—would belong to the farmer, to do with as he pleased.

Amidst the groves of apple trees there rested a stone building which housed the great press and stored the barrels for fermentation. This was the *cidrerie*. Not far beyond there lay a wide lane on which the farmers drove carts of apples to be pressed, day and night, during the harvest season. Between the building and that road was a field where the farmers dumped the waste of the *cidrerie:* cores, seeds, and such material from the presses which was not carted off for cattle feed. This waste was happily consumed by a family of pigs, none of which, unlike the rest of the citizenry, were limited in their rations. Their meat was said to possess the tang of apples, though this may only have been legend.

The traveler approached the wire lattice fence of the pig yard, whereupon a porcine crowd appeared, snorting and grunting, as if to convey some message. She said "Oh, I see. You have no water." She found a wooden tub, dropped it over the fence, and filled it to the brim with a hose from a hand pump. The pigs drank until the tub was dry, then ambled away to lie against the wall of the building.

The hour approached. She circled around the stone *cidrerie* to scan the countryside. It was then she saw the black car approaching from the east. And in almost the same instant, heard the low, dull rhythm of a motor approaching from the west. She knew the one to be a conveyance of the secret police, and the other as the engine of a Westfield Lysander, flying so low as to be invisible amidst the trees.

She watched the automobile attempt to make way to the *cidrerie* down the dirt lanes of the orchards. It rolled into dead ends, turned about, grazed ancient trees, nearly tumbled into ditches—the men inside had not yet realized that they would be better off on foot. Before that occurred, she must find a place to hide. There was no place better than the *cidrerie*; indeed, no other place at all. She went inside, scanned the interior, and scrambled onto the high racks of empty oak barrels. An awful span of time passed before the men arrived, three of them, winded and furious at the exertion.

She knew they were three by their footfalls and voices. One gave the order for the other two to stand at the doorways while he searched the building. The searcher was not dressed for rough work. He could not ascend the press to see atop its structure. This rendered him angrier than before, and an angry man is incautious. She watched as he turned, likely seeking a ladder, and trotted toward the line of stacked barrels.

A cider barrel weighs 50 kilograms, dry. The woman weighed somewhat less than a dry barrel, but she was used to heavy work and had no trouble tipping one over upon the man as he attempted to pass. The blow wrenched his neck sideways and drove his body to the stone floor as a mallet strikes a peg. He said nothing and moved not, but his comrades heard the commotion and came running. They assumed he had fallen and discussed what to do next. While they conferred, the woman sprinted off, feet bounding off the tops of the stacked barrels, until she leaped, fully four meters to the floor, raced down the narrow passage and out the rear door to the fading sunlight.

The sound of her footfalls alerted the men, who sped off after her. The line of the lattice fence was long. She would not be out of sight or pistol shot for at least a hundred meters. And so, on impulse of desperation, she tossed herself over the top stand of the wire and into the enclosure with the pigs. There was nothing to do but run, and a long way to go before the wide span of the cart road—perhaps a lifetime. So she ran, hair flying, with the pigs, roused by the noise and quite annoyed, following behind. Pigs do not welcome trespassers. They quickly overtook her, whereupon she stopped short and lay down. They smelled her all around, looming over like monsters in a nightmare.

At that moment the Lysander's pilot, using up fuel and aware of the hour, set his wheels down at the far end of the long dirt road. The pilot could easily see the woman and the pigs; he could also see the two pursuers, one ahead of the other, as they raced across the field to where she lay.

One of the pigs, perhaps the largest, heard the approaching men, which to him were attackers. He turned upon the leader, who stopped cold, drew a pistol, and shot the pig dead. The pig, however, refused to die at once, and had the thigh of the man clamped in his maw before expiring. The second man sprayed a wild stream of pistol fire in the direction of the pigs, who easily bowled him over to the ground. Pigs who attack people often eat them. The woman didn't see any of that, but the pilot did. He would tell the story for the rest of his life.

The woman would tell only this part: that she boarded the Lysander, shut its canopy, and watched as it sped down the orchard road, taking flight just before a set of cider trees, and in fact barely over them. After that it continued to brush the treetops all the way to the coastline, and then to skim the ocean all the way to England, and then to land, not very far from London; so close in fact that she could take a taxicab to the headquarters of the service to make a report before the clock struck ten. But upon arrival she discovered that the English begin Sunday at sundown Saturday. And that no hotel would admit her at that hour of the night.

And so, the farm woman took a walk through the city. Navigating by memory and by sight obtained from the higher places, she came to a fenced open area, whose barrier she slipped through like a feather; and then found a soft spot, in the place called Hampstead Heath, and fell asleep beneath her cloak.

The Secretary   Michael McGrorty

O n a humid Saturday in June of 1978 I was fading in and out of a
nap at my parents' house outside of Eau Claire after cleaning out
rain gutters. The phone rang on the wall in the downstairs hallway; my
mother answered and said "Phil, it's for you." She expected me to come
right away—I was raised like that—and I did, even though I was 21 years
old.

I stood there shirtless, in dirty jeans, and listened to a man inform me
that I was the executor of a will. He said a few other things, too, before I
could grasp what was happening. My Aunt Agnes died a few weeks earlier.
She never liked to bother people, so we found out after the cremation—a
clever device on her part to prevent folks from spending on air fare. So,
Aunt Agnes was dead: the last of her family, gone in a plume of smoke not
five years after her only brother, my father Gerald.

Two days later a man in a black suit came to the house bearing a sheaf
of legal papers. He explained that I was the executor, and what that meant:
that I was to dispose of my Aunt's possessions, including a little house about
fifty miles distant where she'd lived all her life. At some point I remarked
that this project would entail some effort, to which the man replied,

"Son, you don't understand. Take a look at the papers. You aren't just
the executor. It's all *yours*. You can do with it what you want—house, furniture, everything. There's a bit of value there. You have a year to do it."

I'd just finished my junior year in college and was rather looking forward to a summer of fishing with a beer in my free hand. On the other
hand, the idea of being a property owner—of a furnished house—did
nothing to injure my feelings. I remembered the house all right. It sat
about half an hour distant, outside any town's limits, fairly close to a wide

spot in the Chippewa River where the Pike were big as alligators. That was incentive enough right there.

The next morning, I threw some fishing gear in the back of my pickup and took off for my late Aunt's place. There was nobody on the road but farmers. It had been a while since I was last there—to fix a leak in her roof, as I recall—but there was no way to miss it. A little green two-story in a file of trees, maybe half a mile off the state highway. You turned at a no-name gas station and kept going until the dirt road ran out.

The key was taped to a blank sheet of bond paper in the bundle of documents. I turned the lock; it clicked but nothing happened. Then I remembered that nobody ever went in the front door. It was probably stuck shut. The kitchen door came open easily, and I was struck by the odor of old linen mingled with the musty smell of a house whose windows haven't been opened in days. I took stock of the bottom floor: kitchen; pantry; living room, bathroom, sewing room. All clean and neat as a pin. The stairs creaked and the bannister sagged a little. Whoever bought the place would attend to that. Upstairs were two bedrooms, a sitting room and the usual closets.

It occurred to me that the food in the fridge might have gone south, but when I looked there was only a tub of butter and some condiments. Aunt Agnes had planned for everything. At least it seemed that way until a feathered object fluttered past my face near the pantry. It was a barn owl, and it gave a turn around the living room before disappearing into the hall. The only exit was the attic portal in the ceiling, left wide open. I found a step ladder, fumbled for the light cord and scanned the peaked room for the bird.

Mister Owl glared at me from atop an old hat rack, head bobbing side-to-side like a boxer awaiting a flurry. Unless he had a door key, he had to have come through a hole somewhere. I climbed up and gave him a rush that sent him flapping for a tear in the vent screen. There were no droppings or pellets, so he hadn't had enough time to make himself at home.

The attic was also clean. It certainly would have put the one in my folks' house to shame. And unlike ours, this one had been finished nicely. The sloping walls were paneled, and there were shelves and storage and a bed— made up but covered with a white dust sheet. All in all, it was a pretty nice setup.

The downstairs telephone worked. I called my mother and told her the place was in good shape. She said "Phil, if you get to drinking any beer, you'd better stay there for the night." That's my mother: always thinking. I knew that the little filling station at the highway had nice, cold beer, and drove down to pick up a six pack. The owner and sole employee was there, as he had been every other time I visited. He said "When you get some time, come up and talk to me." I replied "How about tonight? I may not be back for a while." He agreed, saying "I close at eight. See you around then."

Just about eight I heard a knock at the front door, which came open with a hard yank to reveal the gas station man, who introduced himself as Henry Olden. We talked for a while about the fishing nearby, about which, as a seller of bait, he functioned as the local expert. At last he said to me "Look, Son, I got to tell you some things. First off, your Aunt Agnes was my landlord. She owned everything right down to the highway. And on both sides of this house, a full section— mile square, right down to the river. She leased that to farmers either side. You gonna sell this place?"

I admitted I didn't know.

"Well," he said, "if you do, I got to leave. See, I never paid her anything much for the place. She wouldn't have it. Just took it in gas and groceries. The store don't make enough to pay rent anyhow. If it weren't for the tax deductions I wouldn't survive. I just live there and eat—nothing more."

I said "She must have liked you."

He laughed. "Well, we go way back. Our families were real close. I been there since the end of the war. That's when her folks left her the place. They moved to Chicago—gave up farm and all. I was just out of the service and she made a place for me."

"That was very good of her."

"Well," he said, "that was Agnes."

We had our beers and then he left me alone with my decisions. I figured to avoid them until after a session out on the river the next day. I slept on the sofa because it didn't seem right to mess up a clean bed. In the morning I drove down to the highway and picked up some hooks I didn't need from Mr. Olden, who threw in a quart of ale that I probably didn't need, either. On the way out I said "Listen, I haven't made up my mind yet about the property, but I will get to you pretty soon."

By way of reply he said "If you walk to a little old grove of ash trees beyond the fence line there's a drift canoe tied up with a chain."

The canoe was set on the inside of a wide curve, pegged into the bank on a cable so that it would float arrow-straight with the current about five yards offshore. Perfect for casting—but of course, that's why it was put there. I was fishing before my ale could get warm. There may have been pike in the rushes, but I was trying to make up my mind about my aunt's house and didn't focus too hard on what might be biting. After a couple of hours, I tied up the canoe and drove back to the little green house empty-handed.

The downstairs seemed lonely and upstairs the same. The attic felt friendlier; its dormer windows cut the sunlight into a pair of boxes strapped with bars of shade where the muntins held the panes. One of the bright rectangles fell upon a bifold closet door whose handles were old, warm brass. Inside were cardboard boxes labeled with letters: 'A to D,' 'E to H,' and so on. Each was tied with a cord and sealed across its top with a hard-wax seal I was reluctant to break. But it occurred to me that I was their owner, so I cut the tie of the first box, bent open its flaps, and had a look.

They were files of some sort; paper records in thick brown folders, their pages attached by double prongs. The first page I saw was an Honorable Discharge from the U.S. Army for a man named Collis Aspen. What lay behind that was simply the man's military history, from induction physical (subject healthy, afebrile, otherwise unremarkable) to his discharge, going back-to-front in time. The next file was another man's army record, and the next as well. For some reason my aunt had been made, or made herself, custodian of this old paperwork. My initial thought was that it might find a home in some archive—but then I wondered if any of the men in the files might be alive. The paperwork was all duplicates, which meant that the soldiers must have received the originals themselves. There would be no reason to bother them with a mess of carbon copies.

I replaced the box of folders and was about to close the closet when my friend the barn owl thrust himself through the vent screen, veered across the attic, and gave me a sharp rap on the head with his knuckles. After this insult he swung around the room, dove past and into the closet, perching on the last of the boxes. I found a broom and tried to shoo him with its handle, but he dodged every swipe. Finally, as if to mock me, he stood over a wax seal and snapped it with his beak. I took this for a hint of what might happen to my fingers and departed the attic, closing the portal behind.

I was running out of beer but decided to avoid Mr. Olden's enterprise. Having him for a tenant—paying or not—colored our relationship in a troubling way. I felt as if I had been put over a barrel—if not by Mr. Olden, then my aunt. I had suddenly come into possession of a property with strings attached: The land around me was leased to farmers who were likely dependent on its income, and the gas station—well, anyone who took over the property would look for a paying renter right off. I felt like I'd stumbled into a trap.

It seemed like a good time to put some space between myself and the little green house. After all, I could come and go as I pleased, and I needed some time to think. In less than an hour I was back at the family house, waiting for my mother to arrive from work. She found me sitting at the kitchen table, poring over the legal papers that made me the master of a slab of earth along the Chippewa. There was a plat map and surveyor's description, right down to the last foot and angle. There were tax statements, rental receipts, and assessor's valuations. Aunt Agnes hadn't been too severe a landlord: she was extracting about a third of the going rate for farmland in that part of Wisconsin—barely enough to cover the tax burden; another thing I'd have to rectify. My mother's car slid up the driveway and I helped her bring in groceries. She saw me fooling with the paperwork for my aunt's place and said "Put on the teapot and we'll talk."

My mother is from France and likes her tea straight. I take mine with a bit of brown sugar. She opened with "Now you see about Agnes." I said "Not only Agnes, but the whole shebang down there. She's running a charity for her neighbors."

Mom laughed. "That was Agnes. I met her when I was working as a clerk in the army hospital where your father was healing up from wounds in his legs. He was romancing me pretty hard, you know. His sister Agnes was the secretary to the commander of the battalion. She came over with the whole unit and went back with them afterwards. Me, I came back on one of the 'war bride' ships."

I asked her how Agnes might have gotten possession of all the army records of an entire battalion and she said "She just took it on. The men in that group were all her friends. And of course, she was Gerald's sister. You know who you should ask? Hank Olden, the man who runs the store on the highway there. He'd probably know all about it."

So I was aimed back at Mr. Olden, with whom I wished to speak not in the least. That day I received a list of my fall classes from my department. These included a pair of reading lists containing much that was new and difficult. Most history majors are not rolling in money, so I wanted to hit the county library for the books I'd need—and to get a jump on those assignments.

I found about half of what I needed and was about to leave with the bounty when I remembered something from the files in Agnes' closet. I went to the reference desk and asked the librarian, "Can you find me something about Battalion 445? It was an army unit in the Second World War."

She said "Yes indeed. Let me get you our file on that." She returned with a pair of thick folders, saying "You can look at these, but you've got to stay where I can see you. Most of these are originals we can't afford to lose."

I found a table where she could see me and went through the stuff. The first item was a newspaper clipping whose headline read 'Wisconsin Guard Unit Formed from Local Drilling Companies.'

Further on I found an article with the head, 'Battalion 445 to Leave for ETO Soon.'

At the very end of the last folder were pieces on the return of Battalion members in 1945 and '46; in between were pieces on individual soldiers—the sort of stuff intended to boost the morale of the home folks. There was a Battalion newspaper— a double-sheet of mimeographed paper with 'News from the Front' and similar stuff. That lasted half a dozen issues. There was a club of the Battalion's members that held out a good while. It didn't seem like much, overall. I was putting all of that back in the accordion folders when an envelope fell from the stack. It held an invitation to a 'Memorial Service and Luncheon' honoring the battalion in June of 1947.

The card read, "Now that we are home again it is time to take stock and give thanks for what we have. Nine hundred and eighty-seven young men and boys of Battalion 445 left Wisconsin for the fields of war. Three hundred and six returned. Join us in honoring the living and the dead..."

I was no expert on war, but I knew that those were appalling casualties. I handed the folders back to the librarian and said "That was some unit of soldiers." She replied "It was indeed. We may have some materials in the annex. Just ask if you want to see them."

I should have started on my reading for the fall, but Battalion 445 was eating a hole in my mind. Rather than driving home, I turned out and down the highway toward a small green house out in the country.

I stopped to gas up at Mr. Olden's shop. He was busy with a customer. I was going to throw down a buck for a quart of beer and leave, but he said "Hey Phil, I got someone here you need to talk to." The 'someone' turned out to be the tenant farmer to the north side of the road—my tenant. He introduced himself as Jim Slike and said "Oh, I was going over some things with Hank here. Maybe we can go to Agnes' place for a chat." I didn't like the sound of that but they caught me off guard and I told them to come along when they were done in the store.

Half an hour later three pickup trucks came dusting along the little dirt road. One of them was Olden; the other, Jim Slike. The last was driven by Arnie Bullen, the tenant who worked the south side of the road. We sat down in the living room, I poured the beer, and the men more or less gave me the word.

Slike repeated what I already knew: that he was paying rock-bottom for the use of the land; Bullen said the same. They said that they'd had an agreement with Agnes to pay no more than what would cover the taxes and fees— a discount for life. In the middle of this I got frustrated and said "But what did Agnes get out of this deal?"

There was a strained silence before Slike said "Son, she really didn't get much. I mean, we gave her groceries, fixed her car, did stuff around her house. I paneled in that attic—Arnie here re-piped the house. It was just a little exchange thing we had."

It seemed like we were heading to a dead end, so I said "I was reading about the 445th Battalion. They took a lot of casualties."

Slike said "Casualties— more like, everybody died. Seven out of ten, and the rest of them shot or shrapneled or something else."

"Why so many?"

Slike said "That's a long story and a dry one. I got to get home for supper." Hank Olden begged off as well. Arnie Bullen left with them, but gave me a wink on the way out, let them drive away, then came back to the house with a paper bag in hand. He said "I hope you like cold chicken." We ate for a little while and then he said "Okay, now. I didn't want them around to hear this."

He went on. "Back when the war started in Europe, we knew sure as hell it would involve us some way or other. They were putting together all these little high school clubs, you know, doing hokey drills with Spanish War rifles. This county and the ones around it got together in late '39 and got us old doughboy uniforms and boots. There were about 1,500 of us then. In 1940 we had to register for the draft, but nothing really happened and we didn't expect it. See, we were all from farms— they exempted farmers from service. The draft board would to grant you a 2-C exemption if you worked a farm with so many animals and so much in cropland. Well hell, every last one of us qualified for that. Remember, we weren't using that much machinery. It took a lot more people to run a farm than now. So we just stuck around. Lots of us wanted to join, but they turned us down as 'essential to the war effort.' That was how it was. All we did was drill and play war once a month."

I asked how he got into the army.

"Everything changed in '43. See, they were getting to the bottom of the barrel and we were just beginning to fight the war, you know? All of a sudden the governor pressed a button and we were 'federalized.' That was the first step. They told everybody it only meant we'd be getting new uniforms, but you had to know the writing was on the wall. Well, in a couple more months they told us to report for active duty! Some people fought it.

About a third of them got out, mostly because they had nobody at home to work the place, but I got hooked because my Pa and my sisters and younger brother were there. Same thing for Jim and Hank. Big family, off you go. Most of us eighteen, nineteen years old."

"So that was the fifteen hundred."

"Oh, no," he said. "Just about a thousand. They sort of lifted the weight from our parents by telling them that we were to be put into 'reserve' and not used except for work behind the lines. Well, they tried. They invaded Sicily, we got put ashore after most of the shooting and just sort of garrisoned the place. I think we lost two guys to land mines. Then the army got stuck on the way to Rome. Somebody got the bright idea to send us in. See, they were eating up men like breadsticks. We were available, and we went in."

"What was wrong with that?"

"Maybe I forgot to mention. We had no real training. Nothing. The way it usually works is, after boot camp, you get real infantry training, and then you get more in your permanent posting. Well, they assumed we figured out how to be infantry somewheres along the way, only we didn't. That wouldn't have been as big a deal but we weren't added on one and two to a veteran company. They threw us down in our own companies, with green sergeants and officers, right into the Nazis. They ate us up."

"What happened?"

"Everything. My company got moved up in big Willys trucks, split into three groups and sent forward to attack a fortified position that was supposed to have been 'reduced.' It was a concrete bunker, huge thing, maybe hundred yards long, sunk in the ground. They may have shelled it, but they didn't reduce it any. We were told to look for 'embrasures.' I didn't even know what an 'embrasure' was. Couldn't get within a quarter mile. They'd been dug in there for years and we had nothing tougher than a squad machine gun. I tell you, it was like the Civil War—we'd charge up, take our losses, get thrown back, and do it again. After the third time we just quit. My company went in there, nine in the morning, 120 men. Came out at sundown with fifty—most of the rest dead. Only reason I lived was because I was running back and forth to the command HQ.

It was terrible. After they beat us back the last time you could hear them laughing. One guy yelled 'come back, Franklin Roosevelt.'"

I asked "How could it be you got no training?"

"Well," he said, "they figured we were like a National Guard unit, but we weren't. We were just a drill battalion. Our officers hadn't been in the regular army except for a couple. Our colonel was a guy—Addie Berk—who was a big *macher* in Wisconsin politics. Had a lot of money, put together this unit, and pushed us forward until we were into the war."

A thought popped into my head. "What about my dad?"

Bullen rubbed his chin. "Now you know, he was in Baker Company. He didn't go into the first fight. He was in the next one, on the ridges."

"How did he get wounded?"

"Now, don't quote me here, because I wasn't there—but there's no mystery. What the hell, they were just destroyed. It was about ten days later. They pulled them out of a holding position, sent them forward to a set of ridges to spot German movements. I think it was just to wait until they could be thrown into some fight. God knows there wasn't any shortage. Well, they were eating—you have to know how the army did it."

"Do what—eat?"

"No, how they served chow. If you were not up in front you got hot food. Your company cooks made it, then brought it out in cans to where you were posted. That way there's no bunching up. Anyhow, we'd never done anything like that, never organized that sort of line. So when the time came, they all just left their positions except the guards, went to the field kitchen, took out their mess kits and chowed down. Germans saw all these guys standing in one place, sighted in artillery, and hit them all at once."

"And my father got hit."

"Yeah. Got a lot of steel in his legs. I think he was sitting down to eat. About forty got killed, bang, just like that. Lots of wounded. Out of sixteen boys I knew, seven got killed, four got purple hearts. Your dad got sent to the hospital, spent the rest of the war getting back on his feet."

"So where was Hank Olden?"

"He wasn't in Baker Company. He was in Charlie. They had their turn. They were in a convoy of trucks going somewhere, moving everything. Got told to go down one road but the colonel screwed up and sent them down another, straight toward the enemy positions. The Germans shot up the last truck, blocked the road, you know. After that they just picked off the trucks one after another. Another disaster. Guys who got clear of the road went into minefields and were blown to bits."

I didn't know what to say to him—couldn't find any words at all. Bullen grabbed my arm and said, "Now Son, I want you to promise me something."

I didn't know what he wanted, but I agreed.

"You know Jim Slike. He's got the acreage just the other side of me. Do me a favor and don't ask him anything about the war—nothing. It wasn't about him so much, though he got wounded. It was his older brother, Perry. He got killed attacking those concrete bunkers. See, Jim didn't really have to go, but didn't want to have his brother go without him. It just killed Jim, ruined him. He was supposed to go to college but had to stay at the farm after Perry died. So don't mention anything."

"Can I talk to Henry Olden?"

"You can, but I wouldn't. Hank was in Charlie Company. Got stuck in that minefield—saw a lot of his friends get blown to bits. He just laid down where he stood and stayed there until they swept the field the next day. Sobbing the whole time. Lied about his age—he was sixteen when he went over. They had him in the VA for a long time. Finally they let him go. Never could stick with anything. Had all these breakdowns. So leave him be, okay?"

I said "All right, I'll let them alone. But what about you?"

"Oh, there's nothing wrong with me that a little dose of bourbon don't cure. In '46 I got a job in Milwaukee but everything made me, how do you say—*nervous*. Jittery. Too much noise. God damned trains and cars. I gave it a shot anyway but came back here to work my folks' plot, plus the piece along the road near Agnes. I figure to die here if I can."

He looked like he'd said about all he wanted, but I couldn't let him go without asking "By the way, how does Agnes figure into all this? How did she get all those files?"

Bullen replied "They shut down the battalion when the war ended.

Agnes must have saved all the records. See, she kept at it for a while. Took care of us when she could. Nice woman, she was."

With that we parted ways. I watched him roll down the road toward the main highway from the front porch and realized that it was about time for a beer.

Next morning I did what any proper Wisconsin boy does when he needs to think: I grabbed a pole and went fishing. The problem with angling in summer is that the fish don't have to take your lure. There are so many insects landing in any river that your little hooked cricket looks like leftover meat loaf. I could have sworn I heard a nice bass chuckling at me as I sat there getting sunburned, casting over and over, dropping bait in spots where the current promised a nice, deep hole full of dinner. But fishing isn't getting. I gave up after a while and went back down the dirt road.

I drove past the house to the little store on the highway. If I was going to spend any time at my aunt's place I'd need provisions—something more than beer, anyhow. First thing I did was tank up at the pump; after that I grabbed a loaf of rye bread, a dried salami, and a bag of chips. Mr. Olden was there, as usual, wearing a butcher's apron over an old flannel shirt. Middle age didn't look bad on him, but I remembered that I'd never seen him smile. I laid down a twenty-dollar bill and he made change. He said "Bet they weren't biting today. You got to go just about dark. Try some corn. They don't see that falling from the sky."

Back in the truck I counted my money and realized he only charged me for the gas. If that was supposed to make me feel better, it didn't.

I opened the door to Agnes' house and realized that it had become a pretty hot day. I turned on the air conditioning and felt the first blast of cold shoot into the living room. At the same moment, the fan pressure lifted the access panel in the hall ceiling. The board flipped aside and I had to fetch the stepladder to turn it right again. As I reached for the edge, I heard a screech and saw Mister Owl hanging from the attic light cord, rocking gently as he stared at me. At least he wasn't flying in my face, which I took for a positive sign. After a moment he flew a jag across the room, landing on the boxed files. I left to get a glass of water; when I came back he was gone.

The boxes lay waiting for me in the open closet. The one whose seal the owl had broken was unlabeled. Inside were onionskin sheets— copies of correspondence. These were filed by date, with the latest added to the bottom of the pile, prong-clipped together.

I flipped through the stack, expecting to see letters from the formation of the battalion, but the first letter was dated September of 1945—weeks after the war ended. It was from a Major William Callahan to 'Mr. and Mrs. George F. Cohaskey' who lived on a rural route in Dunn County. It began,

Dear Friends,

    I know by this time that you have received information from the War Department regarding the passing of your son, George Jr. I would like to say on behalf of the Battalion and its commander, Colonel Berk, that we share your loss and sorrow.

    Private Cohaskey had all the qualities of a fine soldier and man: he was brave, trustworthy, and honest. He never shirked duty and was ever-ready to volunteer for any assignment. On the morning of September 14th, 1943, he was patrolling the perimeter of our position, searching for enemy soldiers who could penetrate our lines. While on this duty he was spotted and killed by superior forces, but not before signaling the danger to his comrades, which resulted in their closing up the line and saving the position, and many lives.

    Thanks are too small a thing at a time like this, but I would like to extend our heartfelt gratitude to your family for their strength and sacrifice.

God Bless You,
Wm. Callahan, Major, 445th Battalion, U.S. Army

I flipped through the copies. There were well over a hundred of them, each about the same: addressed to the family of a 445th soldier killed in combat. I had no idea whether this was standard procedure or something unique to that battalion. Whatever it was, the letters hit me square in the gut. It was as if I was reading them at the rusted mailbox of some rural crossroads, their contents hard and harsh as a winter wind.

His Company was surrounded by the enemy and pinned down, but Private Clausen volunteered to break out and seek reinforcements. Carrying only his service pistol and three hand grenades, he rushed the line of German riflemen, inflicting significant casualties before he was himself cut down. But his action provided sufficient diversion for the Company to withdraw to safety.

Corporal Williams was on combat patrol when his squad discovered an enemy machine gun nest. Being the senior enlisted man present, he took the initiative, directing that the others surround the gun from either side while he made a frontal attack.

I felt I had split the seal of a shrine, some sacred place. The last box in the cabinet opened and the sacrifice of young men rose to fill the room like a host of phantoms. I read a few more of the letters, lay down on the little bed and watched the sun throw shadows on the fields, longer and longer until the landscape turned gray. It was then I decided to see Mr. Bullen. I had no idea what I wanted to say, but he was the only person I could think of just then, and I needed a man who had been among them.

There was a phone book on the kitchen table; I flipped its few pages until coming to the right name, and dialed. A woman answered. She told me that Arnie was finishing supper but would be glad to see me. I had wanted to have him come up, but she invited me over before I could make the offer. Before signing off she said "You just wait at the fence line. He'll come out and fetch you."

I could see why they didn't want me to drive. The house was fairly close, but right across a wide cornfield that no farmer would want to cut with a road. I saw him leave the house carrying a lantern, then go snaking along a little bear path in the stalks. He came out right in front of me, saying "I can give you some time, but I got to be at an auction at sunup, so we can't throw no party."

It occurred to me, suddenly and perhaps too late, that he didn't want to be reminded of the war any more than Slike and Olden—or maybe he was just worried about whether he'd be able to keep that nice patch of cheap land along the river.

The house was about twice the size of Agnes' place, and exactly like every other farm house in the Upper Midwest: Front door; mud porch; hallway with coat closet. The living room TV set was turned off and a single lamp burned. There was a decanter on the sideboard near two glasses and a bucket of ice. Mr. Bullen said "How do you like your bourbon?"

I said "However," though I didn't know how I liked my bourbon, because I never drank anything harder than beer. I think he might have guessed, because he packed my glass with ice and added a long shot of ginger ale before throwing in a dose of liquor. We sat down just as if we'd known each other for decades, and he said "You get to the end of those files yet?"

I took a mouthful of my drink and swallowed. It was about twice as strong as beer. I said, "Yes. Right to the end."

He drank from his glass, looked down at the carpet and asked "You figure it out yet?"

I thought I'd figured it out, but I didn't want to say something wrong and look stupid. He took a deep breath and went on.

"All those letters are lies. Go back to the files, you'll see. They got sent afterward so's the families wouldn't feel so bad about losing their sons. But not a one of em's true. We didn't have us any heroes in the 445th. Didn't get the chance. Just got mowed down, blown apart. No bayonet charges, no grenade assaults. Nearly every one of those boys died because of some bastard's mistake."

I don't know how long I sat there. It was so quiet I could hear the ice cracking in my drink. Finally I said, "So somebody lied. This—Major Callahan."

"There wasn't any Major Callahan. That's made up too. Agnes wrote those letters. Right there in that farmhouse. She had the stationery and everything. Sent them out to the folks and that was that."

I shook my head. "But why would she take that on?"

"She took on a whole lot more than that. She helped a lot of the guys who came back—got them into college or trade school, helped them file VA claims. She kept the whole battalion together. We had some nice parties for Thanksgiving, Christmas. Agnes was always there."

"Why do you suppose she did all that?"

"Well, two things: that was just Agnes, and, well, you go look up one of those files, for a boy named Joe Millard. Joe was the CO of Baker Company. Your father got hit, Joe carried him to a safe spot, then bled out and died. Joe was Agnes' boyfriend. They were going to get married."

I couldn't think of anything to say. Bullen seemed to know it was time. He said "Give that some thought. Come see me in a few days. We'll get some bait from Hank, fry us up whatever we catch."

The next day I looked for a letter from Major Callahan to the family of Joe Millard. There wasn't any. But there was a picture of him in the files. He was handsome as hell. I stared at it for a while, curled up on the old carpet of that attic, feeling like my own father had just died.

Before the week ended I was out on the river with Bullen, both of us drinking more beer than fishing. He caught a bass that was too small for dinner and was sending it home when I said "Arnie, I want you to do me a favor. Tell Henry and Jim that they're going to have to be a lot nicer to me if they're gonna be my tenants. Oh, and you, too."

I never got around to closing that hole in the attic screen, but I haven't seen the owl in all the time since.

The Carpenter   Michael McGrorty

I was working in my office in the History Department when I got the call from my brother. He said "Perry, this is Alan. Dad died this morning."

The news came as a shock; not because my father wasn't old enough to die, but because I didn't think anything could actually kill him. As Alan gave the details, I penciled out the numbers: he lived seventy-five years—more than my mother by four.

I said "Okay, then. Call Alice and let her know."

My father was a carpenter. He died while building a calving barn for a farmer near Ossipee, the town where he settled after my mother passed away. That was what he would have liked—to die at work. He was a man of work. I seldom saw him idle.

His two vocations were carpentry, and the word of God. The one served him much better than the other, though he persisted in both to the end of his days.

I teach my American Religions students that there is something called 'perfectionism' in Protestantism which expresses itself in the Methodist doctrine of John Wesley, who espoused a formula: sanctification through faith working by love. In my father's interpretation this meant that you got close to God by working like hell at something you enjoyed doing—especially something done for other people. If they don't understand this (and many don't) I tell them to take in their neighbor's trash cans every week without being asked.

My father had his kids take in a lot of other people's trash cans. We also mowed their lawns, sat their babies, and washed their cars. These are things the children of preachers do. They do this so the family may be seen as exemplary. They also do it because the church has always worked within its own network of complementary exchanges: a car wash for a grilled-cheese sandwich; a ride to town for a slab of cake.

My father was born Miller Gable Durand, the second son of a Vermont farmer. His father was not particularly religious. Nor was Miller, known as 'Gabe,' until lightning struck him in his twenties. Before that and after he was a worker in wood. His father apprenticed him to a local builder, who taught the boy joinery and cabinet work in the slow winter months. In warm weather the two of them did anything that needed to be done in the way of farm buildings, houses and furniture. Dad told me that he had "made everything you can make, from wagon wheels to coffins." By the end of the Depression he was ready to become a partner in the firm, but the war came along. The boys he knew were all chafing to join up, and my father, always wanting to show himself an example, had a secret plan. The day his friends went to sign up for the army in Burlington, he took the train to Boston and signed up with the Marines. He held this trick up his sleeve until the others began to accuse him of being a slacker, which he silently endured right up to the night before he embarked for Parris Island.

I have a bootcamp photo of Gabe Durand standing before his country's flag, a sun-burnt, broad-shouldered toothpick. A few weeks more training and he was as ready for war as any 18-year-old could be. He was still 18 when he leaped from the bow of an LCPL onto the sand of Guadalcanal in August of '42.

With the war over, Corporal Durand headed back to Vermont, but found it much changed. His old boss had gone to making wooden boats in Boston. Local prospects did not seem good, so he applied to a vocational furniture-making program at the Parton school in Utica, New York. They were happy to accept him. As it turned out, Parton's new pupil was so far beyond his peers that the staff elevated him to the final year at once, and moreover, permitted him to teach. He quickly became part of the permanent faculty. The pay was small, but he arranged for his degree to be delayed so as to continue receiving G.I. Bill payments. It wasn't, as he told me, a bad setup for a single man.

There wasn't much to do in Utica, evenings, so he stayed in the school, assisting students with their projects. One winter night a car broke down on the street outside their shop. Its driver came around looking for tools. The strangers' car carried a man and a woman, brother and sister, who were headed to a sermon at a Methodist church. Gabe Durand saw that the car would need repairs, and offered to drive them to their destination in the school's van. Gabe drove them there for two reasons: there was no reason not to, and because the young woman was very pretty indeed.

My father was no fool. He knew that he could adjust their carburetor any time, but that the chance to meet a nice young girl should not be lost to mere duty. He sat down in that church, close to the front, and waited. The man spoke first, reminding his listeners of their responsibility to support evangelism in America and other countries—but Gabe was not much interested in that. His eyes were fastened to the girl.

Years later he told me, "Her face was too beautiful for words."

When her turn to speak came, she gave news of her travels throughout the Midwest, especially to poor communities, where help was especially needed; and not only cash contributions, but clothing and "assistance with life's practical difficulties." She said "we cannot be only a church of the book but must be one of the hand and heart as well if our gospel is to take root." She sought volunteers to perform missions— "workers in faith and in fact."

Gabe Durand would later admit that he was not so much interested in working for God as in working within reasonable proximity of that beautiful young woman—or others like her, if the Methodists were carrying a stock. When the meeting ended, he drove the two back to their car, which he then examined before pronouncing gravely that its carburetor required a part which could only be obtained the next day—when it was merely a broken spring he could have replaced on the instant.

Thus the two travelers were forced to take lodgings with friends in the town at a home Gabe drove them to, knowing for a certainty that he would be asked to stay for supper. In my mother's words, "He sat across from me the whole time, staring straight into my eyes. And of course, he was the most handsome man. I didn't know what I wanted more—for him to go away, or for me to go away with him."

The following day the carburetor got its new spring and the two evangelists drove off to another town. But Gabe had not missed his chance. He slipped his name and address into the woman's bag along with a note: "There is a God to seek and I have found Him in your heart."

In the last summer of her life I sat with my mother on the porch of an old stone house in Litchfield. We drank tea and watched a storm wash the countryside, throwing jagged arms of light from the bellies of gray-green clouds. Her eyes were still beautiful, and her smile came again when she said to me "I had it in mind to turn the note over to my brother. I told myself that I would do just that, but when the moment came I couldn't. I sometimes think how different my life would have been if I had!"

My father didn't really expect to receive a response. In fact he hoped that he wouldn't, because that would provide the reason for his next maneuver. Gabe Durand wasn't interested in correspondence with Ida Morten. He was interested in her eyes; in her hands, and the flush of her cheek. None of those things could be sampled through the mail.

At the close of the semester Gabe surprised the faculty by announcing his resignation. He offered no reason, claimed no other employment, because he had none. He'd decided to do two things: pursue Ida Morten to wherever she might be found, and to make sure she never got more than an arm's length away for the rest of his life.

She was about to speak at a meeting in Sedalia, Missouri one warm Saturday, when a tall man entered the rear of the hall, doffed his hat and took a place at the end of the first line of seats. If he thought she would be flustered, he was wrong. She merely began her lecture, as coolly as if the hall had been empty. At the end, she asked them "Who among you will join us, then? Not merely open your purses, but come along, give us a month—two months—to continue this vital work?"

She must have known the result. Among farm people there was much goodness, but very little time, with what time there was dictated by the seasons, the markets, and the animals. They might have time for a charity dance or a knitting-bee, but their other hours were spoken for in advance. The saying was, if a man died in plowing time, they'd bury him between rows, and keep moving.

She stood silently in prayer, as if the Lord would move at least one of the congregation to volunteer; this was better than simply staring at them as they looked anyplace but her direction. And then a voice broke the silence. The man at the end of the front row said "I will go with you, and moreover, I will give you two hundred dollars."

This brought gasps from the crowd—not the promise to volunteer but the vow to provide that much money toward the cause. At that time in Missouri, the average working man wasn't earning fifty dollars a week. Farmers were fortunate to be able to clear two thousand dollars at the end of the harvest year. The handsome then turned the last screw: He approached the podium, opened his wallet, and laid down two hundred dollars in crisp bills.

The room exploded in applause, and even some cheers. After the noise died down, everyone drifted off to the pot-luck, whereupon the lady, now less prayerful in attitude, said to her new volunteer, "That wasn't a request to go with *me*. If you go, you will be assigned a place by the synod."

"If I go," replied the volunteer, "I will go with you, and no other."

"Mr. Durand," she said, "our church does not allow unmarried couples to travel together."

His reply was to smile—the first time she had ever seen him smile, and it had effect. It was a challenge and a promise wrapped in a sunbeam, and she felt the last stone of her footing fall away. She left Sedalia alone, but they were married before the month was out and there was much time remaining to travel in good weather.

The two of them set down to a job whose original incumbent was only moderately successful, despite certain advantages; they themselves enjoyed less success, not only because of difficulties inherent to the enterprise, but because Mr. Durand began to take on more the role of pastor than evangelist, properly speaking.

It was, in retrospect, inevitable. If you knew the man, you would have no doubt of it. Once he had the floor, he became a preacher of a church whose confines were wherever he happened to be. He developed a *following*, to the annoyance of his superiors, who had hoped that he would bring members to the established churches; instead, he became an attraction, eclipsing the enterprise, as it were. It was a thing that could not be tolerated for long, and it wasn't.

By the following spring, Mr. Durand had been disinvited to continue the good work of the synods, which meant that his wife was likewise in a bind. Fortunately, he was able to find work in carpentry, which kept them in groceries and gasoline. They set down in one place and another, doing my father's idea of God's work where it could be tolerated; moving on when it could not.

The problem with the old man was that he painted Christianity with a broad brush. In the Midwest they drew it with a penknife, slicing away everything beyond the borders of current taste and opinion. My parents would be asked to join a particular community of faith, whereupon Brother Durand would cast his spell over the flock, which magic would persist until it began to contrast too much with the former church-and-go-home variety, at which point the couple would be encouraged to try another place, preferably beyond driving distance.

They kept getting rejected across the country, landing someplace for a couple of years, finding little encouraging enclaves whose soil seemed ready for the seed; but alas, my father's doctrines would flow outward and leftward, inevitably leaving the community behind. They were on the road again following the sixth such upset when my mother told Gabe what Mary told Joseph, and they had to choose a place to stay for a long time.

Brother Alan was born in a three-room house that was not so much rented as given away to them in exchange for Dad's labor. This was in New Hampshire, far from the Midwest but not exactly the world center of Christian liberalism. Fortunately, Gabe got plenty of work to support the three of them, first in a window and sash plant, and later in the line of fences, buildings, and barns.

There was nearby a small, private college, ostensibly religious, with a chapel, and a congregation of idealistic students. It was a perfect spot for my father to approach, and he did, with all the charm he possessed. In short order he had become the 'Lay Pastor,' and a father figure to the attendees, who viewed him as a personal embodiment of the Christian Ideal. This was well and good until events in Korea turned to war, and the United States turned to the draft to support its efforts there.

My father had been a Marine, and moreover, a volunteer who lied about his age to enlist. Thus, his response to the war and the draft must have taken the community by surprise, to say the least. At the regular Saturday afternoon meeting of the church volunteer group (all male; clean-cut; most destined for teaching, medicine, or other professions) he asked for time to give a special message about current events. This was granted, and he gave them the first of what became many speeches which, taken together, we came to know as the Guadalcanal Message. Having heard it myself many times over the years, I feel competent to quote:

"Dear Friends, I speak to you today on a subject which has occupied my mind, and very likely yours, for some time now. Events occur which require of men more than an opinion; they call for a choice, for direction; for a form of action. Our times call for behavior based on morality rather than social pressure or the spell of the mob. I refer to the current war in Korea. The decision and the moral choice concern the military draft, to which all of you are likely subject, or soon to be.

As a young man I rode the swell of patriotism, and, with the vigor of youth, joined the Marines in order to fight for Democracy against Fascism. What I got was what every other American who has ever joined the services in wartime receives: an advanced course in killing, a skill attained only after abandonment of mercy and goodness in favor of savagery. Such is the requirement of war and has been since before the Spartans. War requires this—even necessary wars. The Union Armies that won the Civil War did so at the expense of the Southern population; Atlanta had to die and Shiloh burn for that victory.

And so much burning and death occurred on the path to victory over the Japanese. I was barely eighteen when I landed on Guadalcanal. By the end of that battle I was an old man, at least the age of any veteran of Cold Harbor, Verdun, or Thermopylae. The best way to describe it was as endless days of fear followed by sleep-less nights of terror. The Japanese were at least as well-equipped, as ready, and as patriotic as we were. They died in the hundreds, and we died in the hundreds killing them.

I want to tell you that one hour of battle would do great harm to your mind, and to your soul, for life. We lived through weeks of that. We descended to the level of savages, not only to win, but to survive, for a rational, caring human cannot survive war. Only a rational savage can do that. The sooner one made the change the better his chances for survival.

We took almost no prisoners. The enemy who survived and stumbled toward our lines were shot down. Those who resisted, hiding in caves or the brush, were burned or blasted out. The bod-ies of the Japanese dead were left where they lay, or bulldozed into piles and burned.

One night, the Japanese troops made a mass charge toward and into our lines. They came across a hundred yards of open country, screaming, drunk on rice wine, half of them without weapons. We hit them with machine guns and rifle fire, killing wave after wave, leaving them strewn across the landscape. And still they came. The only question was whether we could fire fast enough to kill them all. Some reached our lines, but not many. Have you ever seen a man hit by a machine gun? They do not die like in the movies. They are torn to bits. Pieces of them fly about, and the air is filled with a mist of brains and blood. What does a man become who has done this?

If he survives he becomes a civilian. But not an ordinary man, not ever again. For he has seen and done savage things. He has killed, and even murdered; slain without thought or mercy, and been imperiled so often and so dangerously that his sense of risk and safety will never be aligned with the mind of his youth.

After Guadalcanal I was sent to recuperate from some lung damage I received when an artillery shell landed too close to our position. It might have been one of ours. In any event, I was laid up for about a year, just long enough to be thrown into the invasion of Peleliu. This was, if anything, worse than Guadalcanal. My advantage was that I had already learned how to be a savage. I was wounded again, this time with a bit of shrapnel to a foot. Thus limited, I managed to survive, at least in body. A good number of us were assigned to deal with the dead of both armies. I learned to bury Americans in temporary graves, row upon row, whole or in pieces, without feeling anything more than the ache in my foot and the hot sun on my back. The Japanese were another story. Those we treated with contempt, and why not? To us they were so many dead dogs. Men stole their diaries and pictures, traded for their watches; even their bodies were souvenirs. One man on my burial detail broke out the false teeth of Japanese dead, saving them for the gold.

And of course we knew that more, and perhaps worse, lay ahead. My foot kept me out of the battle for Okinawa, and the war ended before we had to fight a hundred million on the mainland. They sent us home, bid us farewell, and not even we knew what had been lost to gain that miserable acreage.

If my wife were here, she could tell you that I have never had a full night's sleep. My dreams return to Guadalcanal and Peleliu, to the flashes of machine gun fire illuminating slaughter; to the sight of dead and dying comrades; to a war that never ends. Most of us who were there—in the Pacific, in Europe, in North Africa—are probably in the same condition. If we don't speak of it, it's because we don't like to admit that we became savages, that part of us is still there, savage, inhuman, frozen like a scream in a nightmare that will neither emerge nor be silenced.

And so now your turn has arrived. You are asked to join the service, or to submit to a draft process that will send you into the army. I will say this: If you go to Korea—if you participate in that war, which is easily as tough as any of the Second World conflict, you will either die, or be damaged. You may be wounded, but the worst wound will be to your soul. You will have become, for a space of time, without God or even goodness. You will spend the remainder of your life reclaiming humanity, if you can.

I cannot make up your minds for you. I can only say that, if I am called to serve, as I may well be—I will not go. There are alternatives, any of which is better. Not only am I done with killing, I am done with killing my own soul, a thing given to me by a higher power in trust. God bless you all, and good luck."

Those thousand-odd words got my father dismissed from the chapel at the college in New Hampshire, which greatly feared action from the government and moreover, from alumni who had perhaps not been damaged on Pacific islands. He got the sack, returned to being merely a worker in wood, but the problem of his life remained.

My sister Alice came along just about then. My mother remembered that, as with Alan, there wasn't enough money to pay the doctor—and then, somehow, there was. My father was a great scrambler, likely from necessity. If we didn't have money, he'd raise it. Sometimes it took a few entreaties to folks who hadn't paid for work he'd done. The money always seemed to come out of nowhere. 'Providence,' he called it. Waiting for Providence didn't do my mother any good. She said "I was in the waiting room, going into labor, with the admissions clerk telling me that I'd have to pay in advance for the delivery. Well, your father had gone to sell or hock a few things in his tool wagon. He came back with enough cash that I could deliver Alice indoors instead of at the curb."

Somewhere between Alice and me, my parents made a round of moves: to Connecticut, where he worked building vacation homes while my mother taught school; to Upstate New York, where he built barns and a restaurant; then to Vermont, where he sold reclaimed lumber. But these were only money employment. Gabe was, as ever, the pastoral seeker, calling together a flock in some likely spot of the wilderness, then just as inevitably losing it a few months or years later, when the sheep ran him out of the fold.

After the Korean War, my father turned his focus to atomic weapons, which he concluded were an outrage against civilization, and certainly against God's design. Not to mention that they threatened to do to the general population what Guadalcanal had done to him. This was during the Red Scare years, and my father rarely missed an opportunity to denounce McCarthyism along with nuclear armament, in any public venue. On my sixth birthday, I was unwrapping a gift from my grandmother (underwear and blue socks) when I thought I saw a guest arriving. It was a man in a blue sedan, who emerged, took photographs of the cars in front of our house, and drove off. This was the first of the federal agent visits, but not the last. They were there for every subsequent birthday party; for Christmas; sometimes for no reason at all. They'd shadow us as we went to political events or even to church. My father called them 'The Dawn Patrol,' and would often speak to them. He had no hard feelings.

My mother was a different story. I think the scales had fallen from her eyes the second time they got run out of some little township, but she was too busy trying to keep her family on the rails when its engineer was a man suffering from an enlarged conscience. Sometimes they had words. When they had to argue, they would go off for a walk in the woods—we always lived near woods—returning silent, sometimes holding hands, as if some binding pact had been struck among the trees.

But the loss of jobs drove her practically mad. She thought it was my father's friends, the Dawn Patrol; eventually Dad was reduced to working at jobs that were very brief or so concealed that nobody could be pressured to fire him. But then there were the taxes. Every year my parents got audited; every year they were cleared. My father brushed this off but my mother, unaccustomed to war, took it hard.

The last straw snapped when I was in fifth grade and Gabe decided it was time to move to a new neighborhood—to a new set of customers for both carpentry and the Good Work. This New Jerusalem was about fifty miles distant. My mother encouraged him to go. She remained, moored to a fairly decent position in a private girl's school. They told us about it as if it were just a shift in arrangements, but we knew. They would never get divorced, but they would never live together again.

The three of us kids shuttled between them, the two boys spending the most time with Gabe, and especially, through the summers. Alan and

I learned carpentry and how to be a man on my father's curriculum, neither of which involved money wages. The final shift came when we had to decide where to attend high school. Both of us chose my father's district; first Alan, and then me, four years later.

My parents' separation cut the final cord from my father's hands, and he became what he needed to be: a fiery opponent of war and its machinery, especially the military and the draft. When Vietnam flared, he opposed that war with every fiber of his being, spending more time in active opposition to that conflict than he did in paying work. But suddenly he was not alone. Many others, some from conservative churches, came to hear him speak, and a few joined the cause. During those years, Providence, or something like it, bought our groceries and gasoline.

They came to our property, to the great raw-boned wooden barn he constructed with his two sons, to hear him preach. Afterward, the young men would go to the small house and be told how they could avoid the draft. There had to be government agents among them, but nothing they heard was illegal. The problem, for the government, was that it was effective.

Gabe was on a speaking tour in Vermont when he got arrested. The FBI claimed he had transported men across state lines for the purpose of entering Canada to avoid conscription. Their group was halted in a town close enough to the border to make the claim stick. I was reading a high school math assignment when my mother's car came up our gravel drive. She said "Your father's in jail. What do you want to do?" It was my first adult decision. I said "I'll stay here."

They held his arraignment, but denied him bail, claiming he was a "flight risk," and noting that "he refused to discontinue his illegal activities." He waited in jail for a trial. I drove two hours to visit him. He sat behind a rusty wire mesh screen and told me "Don't worry about anything. We'll get by." I asked how he would plead, and he said "I will not make a plea. The court has no moral authority in this matter. I expect to be found guilty anyhow." I said nothing at the time, but drove home angry at him, and disappointed, for the first time in my life.

During that time I took phone calls from people all over the country who wanted to know what happened to Gabe. One afternoon a man from the <u>Union Leader</u> came around and asked "Are you aware that Mr. Durand is facing five years in prison?" I said "I am now. Thank you." And closed the door.

The assigned counsel did what he could, but my father refused to assist in his own defense, and was found guilty, to nobody's surprise. My mother predicted it. On one of our evenings together she said "Gabe always wanted to go down like John Brown, and he will. If not this time, then another. All his effort's gone toward this moment and he won't waste it."

My father's predicament taught me a few things about the law: I learned what 'conspiracy' meant, and that it had the same effect as the offense itself. I discovered that the acceptance or transfer of funds in support of a crime or conspiracy was itself an offense—as was crossing state lines in pursuit of those ends.

I learned a good deal about people, too. During my father's trial, a handful of his followers took the stand to testify that he had indeed told them to do illegal things to avoid the draft and military service, which I am sure was either confusion of my father's message with that of others or outright lies. But it made no difference. My father had reached Harper's Ferry and was bound to free the slaves.

The judge gave him every minute of five years.

Some kindly person in the Department of Prisons sent Gabe to Arizona to serve his sentence. It was a blessing in disguise, because it meant that I couldn't visit him, which I would have done, despite feelings that had passed from dismay to disgust over the course of the proceedings.

Two years passed. I finished high school and was about to make a college choice when I got a letter to report for an armed forces physical. My brother had been exempted because of asthma and one bad eye, but I was healthy as a colt. Shortly after that I got a notice to report for induction. Even so, all I had to do was register for college and I would be safe.

My father was a great lecturer—the best I had seen, or would see, in my life. I heard his words in a hundred venues; not least in the many places where we'd lived. I had the Guadalcanal speech memorized, and that, as much as anything, guided me.

I went for induction and, when they asked if I had any formal objection to service in the armed forces of the United States, I answered "no," Because my father's words told a greater story than the one he intended. They told me about how he had become himself, and I was eager to follow that way to manhood.

I told only my brother Alan, who moved into the house to keep it together until either my father got released or my own term expired. The army sent me to boot camp and then informed me that I'd qualified for a number of technical jobs, some of which would keep me from actual combat. I turned them down and said I wanted to be in the infantry. The army, not surprisingly, had no problem satisfying this request.

Vietnam was not a set-piece war of massed armies or choreographed invasions. We fought small groups and even individuals, in nameless engagements that usually took mere seconds to resolve. Our opponents were seldom well-trained troops. Most of the time they were teenagers—sometimes barely that. But they could kill, and our work was to kill them.

The second difference in our war was that we did not fight for territory, or to take capitals. We fought to extinguish opposition, to exterminate as many as possible and scatter the rest until we could kill them, too.

Some of our strategies were poor or misapplied. We had the advantage of airpower and armament, but they knew how we would operate. Moreover, they were satisfied to inflict damage and retreat into hiding. Both sides believed they could discourage the other—a fundamental error in war, which assumes the enemy is morally weaker.

In my Vietnam year I made nineteen forays into enemy territory, most of which resulted in nothing whatever. We would be brought in and dropped where the enemy had been sighted or were expected to appear. Nothing tips off the enemy like a helicopter. Usually they would have faded into the landscape by the time we got into our patrol. On a cool winter day in 1968 these arrangements were turned about, leading to a different outcome.

Nothing is harder to navigate than a landscape of rice paddies. They all look the same from the air, and the rivers that flow along them have few distinguishing features. They are only dark green ribbons winding along a skewed patchwork of lighter-green puddles. We trusted our pilots to know where to put us. Their mistakes were frequent, but usually fortunate, setting us too far from the enemy. On that day they erred to the opposite extent, making up for all the times we'd been left to do nothing until sundown.

The drop point was supposed to be within a river's tight curve, from whose neck we would emerge to seek the enemy in the open country beyond, using the dikes as pathways. The problem was, the river was a snarl of oxbows like a plate of spilled spaghetti. Somebody chose the wrong loop, and that made all the difference.

We were set down in the belly of a wet circle. Our pilots chose that spot rather than an adjacent river loop because the other was stacked with sheaves of rice straw. A few seconds after the Chinooks were over the horizon, the sheaves erupted in spurts of flame. The AK-47 has a distinct sound, and the M-16 another, but their bullets sound about the same. I heard the North Vietnamese guns fire for about ten seconds before the first M-16, which may have been mine. That any of my company survived the first few seconds was because the enemy—not the bare-chested Viet Cong but the full-powered North Vietnamese Army—was taken by surprise. In fact, they were in the same bad situation as their opponent: caught in a ring of muddy soil without real cover, in full sight of the enemy. Their only shield was the same as ours: a waist-high mound of dried mud on their side of the riverbank, only a few feet wide.

Draw a two-lined 'S' in your mind. Push down its ends so that they nearly touch the center bar. Put two armies in the loops. That bar was our mutual objective. For either of us to win, or to escape, he would have to take the line of high ground on the other's side of the river. One of us, the Americans or the NVA, must reach the opposite ribbon of high ground first, and alive.

Their first rounds caught a few of us; the rest fell flat, below the level of the dike's edge. Our sergeants shouted orders, but it was obvious what had to be done. The dike was about fifty yards away. This would be covered at a stumbling crawl, to keep below the mud shelf and the bullets that were already shredding its ragged grass.

Very shortly I also heard the crack of the NVA machine guns, and the faster pounding of our M-60s. But they were both shooting at the sky;

their targets had gone to ground, creeping like mad lizards toward the pair of mud ribbons dividing them.

The distance to the dike took me a few seconds. I turned at its base to see dozens of men straining to close the gap, and, scattered among and behind, stragglers—some dead, some dying, some being struck as I watched, arms jerking and legs collapsing as a bullet found them. In a weird reversal, the medics dragged them *toward* the enemy. In less than a minute everyone alive on either side was huddled against that barrier.

We had a lieutenant named Griggs calling the tune that day. He made the choice that determined the outcome. He ordered us to form two groups at the flanks, forty yards apart, and wait. As we crawled to our positions he chose ten men to remain in the center.

The hand grenade was made for times like that. We knew they would be using them because that would be our first choice, too. And quicker than you can say it, the NVA began to rain grenades over the dikes. These were of the wooden-stick type, and they didn't do much damage. Most fell short or long. The grenade is a prelude to a charge, but there was no charge from their side. Then we were ordered to throw our own grenades. Dozens went over, followed by a satisfying chorus of blasts. At that moment I saw the lieutenant and his picked cohort disappear over the edge of our dike. Had I been willing to risk my life, I would have seen them ford the muddy lane of water, no deeper than a knee, and take cover beneath the opposite bank.

With that we were ordered to toss another shower of grenades, and then to follow the lieutenant's group across the water. We did so, throwing random bombs and firing at the top of the bank until finding cover. The NVA guns were mysteriously silent. None of us saw they had made a run for the distant neck of their oxbow.

At a signal our three groups took up positions on the NVA dike, but found that the enemy had taken off through the maze of sheaves. We should have stayed in position, waiting for orders, but savages surrender to instinct. Nearly all of us ran forward, firing into sheaves, soldiers, or shadows, rolling up the NVA troops from three sides until the survivors could only head across open land toward the far bank. The ones who did were cut to pieces by machine gun fire. They streamed across the paddy until the streams of bullets turned them into broken dolls.

Our company ran a rough circle around the field, killing the last of the living. Many of them fell inside or near the rice straw, which caught fire and burned. We made no effort to stop the flames. When the Chinooks came to get us the loop was a circle of smoking embers and charring bodies.

If my son asks me, I will tell him that I killed three men that day. The first was an NVA soldier who was lying on the wet ground, firing on our platoon. He was a brave fellow, making time for his comrades to escape. I fired into his blind side; he let go his rifle and died. The next was an officer who knelt at the base of the mud dike. He had been wounded in the leg and couldn't walk. I shouted at him *"dau hang!"* but he looked at me with sad eyes and raised his pistol. I shot three holes into his shirt and he slumped to the ground.

The third man I killed was the last member of Gabe Durand's family entourage. I didn't know that until one night in a Saigon bar, when the waiter who brought me my beer looked exactly like the man I'd killed beside the river dike. That vision began a cascade of difficulties which I have fought and compromised with ever since.

I got released from active duty in California, and went straightaway home. In a few weeks I was enrolled in college, looking from the outside like every other undergrad, though perhaps a bit graver in aspect. The draft was over and the war soon to end. The papers were full of the *My Lai* court-martials and I wanted nothing more than for my own memories to fade into the background of civilian life. Gabe Durand was released from prison that year, just in time for Christmas. He arrived at the Manchester bus station wearing a trench coat that hung so loose he looked like a scarecrow. We embraced and I thought I could feel every one of his ribs. I remarked that he was thin and he said "Fasting for the cause. Purifies the soul."

I drove us to a road house for dinner. He refused to speak about prison other than to say that he was the only war protester in the facility. I asked what he planned to do. He said "Carpentry, and keep on against war." He never asked how I had been, or about any of the family. I know that Alice had written to him, but he never mentioned it. That evening, just before bed, he said to me "I know about your army time. I don't reject you for that. Every man comes to his own conscience a different way."

When he left for prison I'd been a boy but now I was a man, in another man's home. I didn't want to live in Gabe's house because it wasn't mine and I didn't want to be anybody's son just then. After the holidays I got a place near school and stayed there except for visits to my parents in their separate houses.

My father's foot began bothering him to the point where I had to drive him to the VA for treatment. I heard the doctor say to him, "Mr. Durand, it seems that your shoulder had been broken some time ago. How was this?" Gabe replied "Oh, I was along the Jabbok, wrestling with an angel." He was more straightforward with me later: "I was preaching in the prison yard and some nice bank robber didn't like my sermon."

The shoulder, the foot, and advancing age made it harder for Gabe to put together houses, but he never quit. We worked together in the summers. The new money wanted country homes that looked as if they'd been hewed from timber. We built those frames and left them to be finished by others. On cold winter days I'd look out my classroom windows to an icy patch of ground and think of him, barehanded, planing planks and cutting tenons.

After graduate school I began looking for a teaching job. I'd applied all over the country with no success and was about to chuck it all in when I got an interview with a small college quite close to home. The committee was composed of two men and two women, all of the worn-tweed variety. They were looking for somebody to teach the History of Western Religious Thought. I gave my presentation, which I feared was weak. Afterward they bought me a consolation lunch at the town pub. At the end, one of the men took me aside and said, "You're Gabe Durand's son. I remember you from the draft meetings." To my surprise, they hired me.

My father gave me his house and settled down in Ossipee, sometimes living in a half-built place, other times renting a room from friends. Gabe never ran out of friends, just as he never ran out of money: whenever he was in need, Providence opened its purse.

The last time I saw him was the month before he died. It was May—high spring in New Hampshire. I brought him a set of chisels that I'd gotten at an auction. My last memory of him will be of the two of us squaring window frames beneath a budding oak.

He died unburdened as a hermit. Apart from tools there was only some worn clothing, his boots, and a footlocker; no more than would fill the back seat of my car. I was carrying the locker to the basement of Gabe's old house when its hinge gave way; I ended up with the lid in my hands and the bottom half on the stone floor. There, inside, was a uniform, an army helmet, and a green glass jar half full of gold teeth.

Confidence Man   Michael McGrorty

B oxing may be the most misunderstood activity on earth. People who
witness a boxing match come away with various impressions, but the
truth is that boxing is nothing less, and very little more, than an expression
of confidence, and this is only known by those who have worn the gloves.

Everything I know about boxing was taught to me in the Navy by a
fellow named Tommy Rasher whom I met in the early twilight of a naval
career that was only just starting when the Japanese decided not to call our
bluff on that third A-bomb. Both of us were serving on an old transport
known as the *Hennepin County.*

On a sweltering August night in San Diego the luck of the draw put
us together on shore patrol. Tommy wasn't the talkative type, so we passed
most of the evening quietly walking circles around the bar district beyond
the base gates. We were leaning on a parked car across the street from a
country-western dive called The Lariat when two fellows tumbled through
the curtained doorway, swinging at each other. I can still see Tommy, a
small fireplug of a man, striding over to where the two drunks were rolling
around, pushing up the sleeves of his dress whites as he walked. By this
time, the bigger of the two combatants, having gained a sitting position
on the torso of his opponent, was raining unanswered blows to the other
drunk's face and head.

What happened next was quick and memorable: Tommy had no
sooner arrived at the scene than he simply took the big man by the hair,
pulled him upright, and announced, "The fight's over, now get the hell
out of here." At this, the drunk took a swing at Tommy—actually more
of a roundhouse right, his arm sweeping majestically overhead as Tommy's

right hand, then his left, were buried in the big man's stomach with a noise like a thumped washtub.

The whole thing couldn't have taken fifteen seconds. My shipmate hadn't even lost his hat. Tommy walked back across the street and said, "Let's move on before we have to explain this." I was full of questions and barely suppressed admiration, but he did nothing more than mumble until we were back on the ship, eating a midnight breakfast on the empty mess decks.

"That was pretty nice boxing," I volunteered. Tommy simply frowned, slashed a fork through his egg yolks and said, "Punching out a drunk isn't boxing. Boxing is nothing like that." I finished my breakfast without another word, and woke up the next day still not knowing what boxing was, but determined to find out.

Over the next few weeks I maneuvered myself into Tommy's company on several occasions, but never managed to ask him about boxing, or anything else. His very presence intimidated me, and there were other things that kept my tongue tied: He was a Machinist's Mate, First Class, and I merely a Third-Class Yeoman. We had absolutely nothing in common except that we both breathed air and served on the same ship. Aside from that, he was an Old Navy type, right down to the tattoos, a man for whom the service was a way of life. He was perfectly at home in the infernal atmosphere of the main spaces and had the respect of the men above and below him. I on the other hand was a green city kid for whom the Navy was a good way to avoid the infantry while reading novels. I did approach him a couple of times as he sat eating dinner, but he froze my courage with a flinty glance and I managed only a hello before heading back to work.

Then, one day after dinner, as I sat reading the newspaper in the shade of the port gun tub, a figure approached with the sun at his back and said in a gruff voice, "Have you got the sports pages?" Shielding my eyes, I looked up into Tommy's ruddy face and lied, "Sure, I'm all finished with them." To my astonishment he sat next to me and read through the section. In the few minutes he was there I rehearsed about three hundred casual ways of expressing my interest in boxing, but before I could begin, he said, matter-of-factly, "I'm heading out to coach some kids at the lodge hall down on Paterson Street tonight. Come along if you like."

At knock-off, he appeared on the quarterdeck with a seabag full of boxing gloves that he transferred to my custody. I'd never touched boxing gloves before; these were the laceless type used for training. They smelled like the back of an old taxi.

The lodge hall was an ancient building that had seen considerable use as a rental hall for dances and weddings, but its best days had passed with the Charleston. The surrounding neighborhood must have been classy at one time, but had passed "shabby" on the way down decades before. By the time I saw it, the hall was being rented at ten bucks a night to the city's Parks Department, which, in keeping with tradition and conventional wisdom, offered boxing to the offspring of the poor.

Tommy rounded up his group of boys, who ranged in age from nine to twelve, sending them out to run around the block. While they were gone, he told me how I could help, which was mainly by staying out of the way. When the boys returned he divided them into groups of three and set them to work punching heavy bags. A half-hour later he took them aside one at a time, and had them throw slow punches at him as he countered with slow punches of his own. After more heavy-bag work he paired the boys off to spar, each wearing oversized gloves and enormous padded headgear.

It was all over in two quick hours. My help had consisted only of holding the heavy bag and gathering up equipment. But when the last kid had left, Tommy turned to me and said "Now put on a pair of gloves and I'll show you a few things."

What he showed me, as gently as possible, was that he could hit me anywhere, anytime he wanted, and that, try as I might, I couldn't touch him. It was my first lesson in what some ringside observer—who obviously had never put on the gloves—once called "the sweet science."

Over the next few weeks I helped Tommy with his young charges, at the same time learning the fundamentals of boxing, beginning with the visceral reality that boxing is, first and foremost, *painful*. The mechanics of the sport are simple enough—any schoolboy can imitate a boxer's stance and technique. But beyond mechanics there is the unavoidable truth that while your object is to strike your opponent with as much force as possible, he has the same idea. Add fatigue to pain, and a boxing match becomes more a thing of strategy than of brute force.

Before going into technique, Tommy made sure that I understood the elements of pain and fatigue. The first month he had me jump rope for a minute, then defend from a fixed position another minute, then attempt— vainly—to reach him with punches. After a month he began teaching me when to use and anticipate certain punches. For a while I got better, but then seemed to stall. I became frustrated, and when one night it seemed my mentor was being unnecessarily thorough, I got mad and cursed him: whereupon he stood back, laughed, and said, "Now listen to me. Your arms are six inches longer than mine. If you'd put your goddamned hands up and throw *straight* punches, you wouldn't be getting beat so bad."

He was right, of course. At the time I spread 150 pounds over a six-foot frame, with long, wiry arms. Tommy couldn't have been more than five-foot-seven. Although he was certainly more skilled and experienced, I should have been able to keep him at bay, but instead had been fighting inside, toe-to-toe, where his short arms gave him an advantage. On the drive back to the ship I asked him why he hadn't corrected me earlier. He told me I hadn't been ready. I wanted to drown him.

After altering my technique I seemed to improve—at least Tommy wasn't beating out a drum roll on my head. I was even snapping off a good combination from time to time. Buoyed by this success, I decided to take on the world, and asked Tommy if he might set me up with a three-rounder at the smokers the following week.

Smokers are as old as the Navy itself. The term signifies the informal (and often illicit) boxing matches held aboard Navy ships and shore stations. Smokers were originally used as a forum for settling disputes between shipmates. According to tradition, the aggrieved parties don gloves and take swings at each other until one party cries uncle. Seldom is anything like real boxing skill exhibited in these grudge matches. On larger shore bases, smokers take on the formality of amateur boxing and lose the grudge match aspect altogether—though the level of performance isn't that much better.

My introduction to the ring took place at the San Diego Naval Training Center, familiar to thousands of former Navy men as boot camp. Having been a boot there, I had a pretty good idea of what lay ahead: an outdoor ring set up inside a square of ancient wooden bleachers, and a three-round tussle with some inept recruit who'd probably been put up to the match by his pals.

So it was on a cool October evening I stood face to face with another skinny kid named Kessler, touched gloves and entered the world of boxing.

Poor Kessler. Maybe he had been a terror to his little brother, or had watched too many boxing newsreels. In any event, he didn't fare well. His initial offering was a roundhouse right that I ducked, countering with a right lead to the stomach and a left to the head that sat him down hard, more from shock than any real injury. Rising, he decided to adopt something along the line of an orthodox boxing stance, poking a tentative left ahead of a right hand held too low to protect him. Remembering Tommy's lessons, I snapped two lefts at his eyes to gauge distance, then shot a right hand to his face. A moment later, Kessler sat honking blood through a broken nose, likely to fight no more.

For me, however, there would be other smokers, one each weekend, until they became so predictable that Tommy quit coming along. Most of the time I was matched with duplicates of Kessler, but occasionally I saw an organized defense, and sometimes got hit with a punch that rattled my brain; but Tommy had been a good teacher, and before I knew it, I'd won fourteen fights, most by knockout. I might have gone on like that forever, but the Chief Petty Officer who ran the smokers let me know that I'd be boxing at a ten-pound handicap if I wanted to keep knocking down people on Saturday nights. There was no way I could have handled anyone that much heavier. It was his way of telling me to move on to something else.

Although I didn't realize it back then, Tommy had taught me boxing in a way that overcame the first and most fundamental of boyhood fears—that of being hit by someone else. Like most younger siblings, I grew up under the tyranny of a big brother who could and did thump me whenever he felt like it. Fighting—that is, standing up and returning blows—was out of the question. I was always younger and smaller, and giving up the chocolate bar was easier than getting a black eye. Over the years, I'd lost confidence in myself. But Tommy taught me the first law of survival: one can deliver blows as well as receive them.

Slowly, imperceptibly, Tommy had restored my confidence. I realize now what a good heart he must have had to take me in, to waste hours on a kid anyone could have seen would never become a real boxer. I real boxer, I would learn, was a guy who had never wanted for confidence, hit harder than his weight, and defended well enough to be around to hit back. Hank Sanborn was a real boxer.

Hank was a welder on the base who'd trained under Tommy for a couple of years. At 160 pounds, he was a middleweight, and he fought in real fights, the ones held downtown at the veterans' hall, or in preliminaries to bigger fights out of town. Tommy found Hank a few years before, trimmed him down, and taught him to keep the cork in the bottle. Since then Hank had about a dozen fights, mostly eight-rounders, winning all by knockout. Despite being close in weight, I would never have thought to spar with him. I'd seen Hank knock a man out by driving the man's own glove back into his face with a punch. As a boxer, he was going places.

For a long time I didn't seem to be going any place in particular, but after an eternity of pestering I got Tommy to arrange for my entry into the regional tryouts for the Navy boxing team. Basically it was an amateur hour for aspiring pugilists, most of whom had about my level of skill and experience. But not all, as I found out.

The tournament rules would be different and, it seemed, in my favor. Avoiding a punch counted as much as delivering one, and I'd been taught to be a good avoider. In my first fight I jabbed and poked my way past a guy who spent his time loading up for a big punch he never delivered. In a second bout, five hours later, I ran into trouble, getting cracked repeatedly by a Puerto Rican with a penetrating jab and a habit of butting with his head. By the third round I was on my way to losing when my opponent butted me once too often and was disqualified. Tommy didn't even look up when I walked back to my corner. On the following day, Easter Sunday, I was knocked senseless by a fellow I had no business being in the ring with.

No business whatever. Before the match Tommy told me this fellow had fought something like two dozen amateur bouts, and he could handle himself. He also told me to circle away from his right, and not to let him set up for combinations. What he didn't tell me was that the guy had only missed making the Navy team the previous year because he'd punched out a couple of military policemen.

At the end of the fight I knew how they must have felt. From the first bell I was dodging and covering up, trying to establish a rhythm, while my opponent was jackhammering my arms and shoulders, looking for an opening. Trying to salvage the first round, I threw a right lead which he answered with his left, coming just over my glove like a hawk diving on a pigeon. It took about a tenth of a second, but I can still feel that punch landing. Lightning exploded in my head and my legs went limp. My tournament was over.

I stayed away from Tommy for a while after that, from anger and shame. Anger because he hadn't told me the truth; shame because of the way I'd found it out. Tommy taught me that boxing was about confidence, but confidence wasn't always enough. In the world of ordinary men the confident would prevail, but among the confident, other rules applied. The knowledge hurt: I would always be better than the average man with my fists, but never a competitive boxer.

Gradually the pain of the lesson eased and I drifted back to Tommy. I ran with the young boys and hit the heavy bag, but most of the time was devoted to preparing Hank for his fights. Other things came along to fill the void: I got accepted to college, bought a car, and began counting down the days to my discharge.

Tommy seemed to change as well. We had long talks about boxing, the Navy, life in general. One night, after a pitcher of beer, he told me that he'd been a fighter before becoming a boxer. As a minister's son growing up on an Indian reservation, the only white kid for miles, he was a natural target for abuse. "By the time I was fifteen," he said, "there wasn't a man around that could beat me, and only one person I was afraid of—my older sister, Clara." He'd qualified for the Navy boxing team as a featherweight, but was forced to quit when his hands, broken in too many childhood fights, refused to mend.

Tommy admitted he had no hope of seeing Hank develop into a premier boxer. He had recently passed the board for Chief Petty Officer, and would advance in a few months. That would mean a new ship, and no chance to train boxers. Whatever impact he might have on anybody would be soon, or never.

In the time remaining he wanted to expose Hank to variety of opponents before sending him off to a professional manager. Then came a shocker: He asked if I'd take time to spar with Hank between workouts. Before I could answer he said "The only reason I ask is that you have fast pair of hands, and I think Hank should get used to seeing some speed."

Speed I had, but no power. Hank had a knockout in either hand, but I had about one knockout divided between right and left. The power I didn't have was the thing that confidence could not make up for, and that made the difference between me and guys like Hank.

To get anywhere as a boxer, Hank would have to become available for longer fights, and he'd have to train accordingly. Tommy had him run through a tough workout six nights of the week, and after nearly exhausting him, would have him spar with me for five rounds. Hank wore conventional headgear, heavy oversized gloves, and a three-pound weight around each ankle. I wore a large headgear and a padded singlet. The idea was to make it a tough proposition for Hank and to keep me from being killed.

Hank's style was to bombard his man with punches. Tommy's idea was to break him of that by fatigue—to keep him so tired that he'd learn to conserve his power for the late rounds. It wasn't easy on either of us. Poor Hank looked like a crippled dinosaur, staggering around trying to get at me. Poor me when he did—he'd come right through my jabs like Sherman through Georgia, then lean me into the ropes and bang away until my ears buzzed. For a long time I went to bed with the taste of blood in my mouth.

After a few nights of this I learned that the only way to avoid a headache and purple eyelids was to keep Hank in the center of the ring, crack off a couple of punches, then leave town before the storm hit. Hank's strategy was to cut off the ring and prevent my escape. He was successful enough to make me find ways of getting out from under, but I was forcing him to discriminate, to wait to pull the trigger. It was satisfying in a strange sort of way.

Like any other sport, professional boxing is a public entertainment that has to appeal to the crowd beyond its circle of cognoscenti to pay the bills. This means that promoters are more likely to feature the boxing equivalent of Babe Ruth than a great defensive fighter. The record books are full of boxers with excellent skills who never made any money for themselves or their managers. Ask any man to name three famous boxers, and you'll get a short list of knockout specialists. If he mentions Benny Leonard or Willie Pep, you've run into a real fan, if not a historian. Knowing this, Tommy set Hank up with six-round matches designed to show off his punching skill and potential as a gate attraction.

Hank fought three times in two months, knocking out everyone he met in the first round. One fellow he hit with a nasty hook was out cold for a whole day. I remember the guy's mouthpiece flying out, landing three rows deep in the seats. Hank received the princely sum of fifty dollars for each fight, of which Tommy took a third, giving me half his share. Finally, Tommy he was approached by some folks from Los Angeles interested in buying Hank to turn him into a full-time pro.

It says a lot about Tommy that he agreed to sell his interest only after ensuring that Hank would get a decent contract. It says even more that he gave Hank half the five grand he was paid, and that he wanted to give me a couple thousand for working out with Hank. But that was later on.

Before settling the deal, our friends from Los Angeles decided to test the mettle of their prospect by putting him against a known quantity. This was a delicate matter to arrange, since having Hank face a really tough opponent at that point might end in a loss that reduced his market value. Their solution was to have Hank fight under an assumed name, in a private club fight in an out-of-the-way place.

Tommy agreed to have Hank go six rounds with a former middle-weight contender named Joe Maxwell. In his day (which passed a decade before) Maxwell had been ranked as high as tenth in the country, but the reason for the present matchup was that he could take a terrific punch. Hank's job was to deliver enough terrific punches to convince our friends to sign him up. The situation looked good, but there was one catch. They needed another fighter for the card.

The club in question provided boxing to its patrons more for gambling than entertainment. More matches meant more bets, and more of a cut for the house. The club operators required at least two matches from each manager. Hank told me this because Tommy wouldn't, knowing I'd jump all over him to get into the ring. He was furious with Hank for having told me, but calmly recited the argument against my fighting on the undercard: I'd get the hell beaten out of me, if I wasn't actually killed, by any club fighter on the planet. With only three months left on my enlistment and a world of possibilities waiting, why do it?

Because I wanted one last fight, I told him. Because I'd trained with Hank and could take a punch. Because there was no time to find another boxer. Finally, and persuasively, because he could throw in the towel if I got into trouble.

So it was that I found myself preparing for a six-round fight with an unknown opponent, to be held someplace I'd never heard of. But I wasn't worried. At the time, my greatest concern was keeping my girlfriend from finding out that I was boxing. This wasn't easy. It's hard to kiss someone convincingly with a split lip, and even harder to explain scratches on your back left by the ring ropes.

I probably couldn't pull it off now, but at twenty all things were possible. I don't remember thinking about whether or not I'd win the fight; to me it was simply a chance for a last hurrah. Hank was the guy with all the problems.

On a cool spring evening we set out for our rendezvous, three adventurers in a borrowed car. Hank had been so focused on training that he'd never inquired where he was to fight, and I didn't care enough to ask. With Tommy behind the wheel, we drove about an hour east of the city, beyond the realm of streetlight and sidewalk, gradually losing the houses, turning down narrower and narrower roads, until the headlights shone on vacant lots, then scattered farms, then on endless ranks of citrus groves intersected by eucalyptus windbreaks. Finally, railroad tracks, a sharp turn, and in the distance, an ancient wooden building squatting like a grounded ark at the margin of a muddy field.

Tommy pulled up beside a battered loading dock that seemed a mile long. Farther down the dock other cars had stopped; here and there little knots of men stood smoking, drinking from bottles, waiting for something. Tommy cut the ignition and lights, leaving us some distance from the others. After a few moments of chilly silence he said, very softly, very slowly:

"Mack, you are to fight a man named Tanner. He does work as a pipe-fitter when he can find it. I would guess he's about thirty-five. Years ago he was a lightweight, but he's drunk his way up to your class. Listen carefully now: He's an old man and a drinker, but he's very tough and can hurt you. He only comes here when he needs money. He and everyone else will be betting that you can't go six with him. Whatever happens, don't let him get inside or pin you down."

To Hank he said only "You remember what I told you."

We grabbed our gear and climbed a flight of wooden steps to a sliding door at which a figure in a dirty windbreaker waited. We paid him a dollar each and passed inside.

We had entered a fruit-packing house, a huge old barn which bore the character of everything that had ever been shipped through it and the odor of anything that the local dogs dragged through in the slack season. The effect was of the great hall of a barbarian king, with traces of the Augean stables. Above a concrete floor littered with orange wrappers and crate-nails arched a maze of dark timber rafters from which a circle of gasoline lanterns was suspended. The lamps hissed and cast the room in a cold, unnatural light. Beneath them was the ring, unfamiliar at ground level, its two-strand ropes threaded through block posts sunk into the cracked floor. Beyond the range of the lanterns in a cool twilight darkness stood a loose circle of men, not drinking, not smoking, talking very little, waiting to box one another.

Hank stripped down to his trunks, and while Tommy taped his hands I walked with what I hoped was a purposeful stride over to the group beyond the light. All five were dressed in street clothes and had the broad-shouldered look of boxers, except that they all seemed, well, too old. Joe Maxwell looked fully a decade older than Hank, and the others seemed to have some miles on them, too. Finally I asked, "Where's this Tanner fellow," which brought a chuckle from a few throats. Maxwell said, "He's over at the door, the one taking tickets. Must be behind on his bills again."

I couldn't believe it. The man who took our tickets! He looked to be about forty, with some hard years mixed in: five-foot six or seven, with thick hands and a battered brawler's face. His windbreaker was torn, his hair dirty, his shoes pitiful. I felt sick, then angry. My last match, against this shabby old man! I turned and stormed back to Tommy, who was just finishing up with Hank.

Tommy never looked up. "Before you say anything, you'd better know that he's never been knocked out here, and something else—he's fighting for bread. You're here because you don't know any better. Maybe if he goes six, he'll get his toolbox out of the pawnshop. Now, strip down and let's tape you."

There were three fights before mine. Hank's was the second. As the first fight got underway, the crowd of about a hundred men settled in atop stacked pallets and crates. Everyone smoked, and most were drinking. Tommy explained the arrangements: At the end of the first round, bets would be placed as to the winner, the final round, and whether one or another man could go the distance. The house got ten percent of anything under a hundred, and five percent above that.

The first fight was something of a let-down with an energetic light-heavyweight knocking out a lethargic one in the third round. The referee was satisfied to count the loser out from the comfort of the far corner, where he'd stood, leaning into the ropes, for the entire fight.

Hank's fight was something special. Maxwell tried to get him to brawl, but Hank stood back and placed his shots carefully, countering through a storm of wild punches and landing about every other punch he threw. By the third, Maxwell was in trouble, and was lucky to survive the fourth. He failed to come out for the fifth, which earned him a chorus of curses and a hard shower of assorted coinage. Hank was ecstatic, and Tommy managed something like a smile. From across the ring two men rose and, calling to Tommy, gave a thumbs-up and left the place. Hank was on his way.

I don't remember the next fight, but I do recall looking at Tanner through the ring ropes. He'd stripped down to trunks and shoes, and was wearing a sweatshirt that might have doubled for a grease rag. Finally, when everyone had settled up, the referee signaled to us and I took my corner with Tommy. Across from us Tanner stood alone, without handlers, middle-aged, with a trace of a gut and a farmer's tan over a sallow complexion. He didn't seem to be in fighting shape, but his arms looked as hard as stone. The referee waved us both to the center of the ring, Tommy whispered "Okay now," and I went forward to meet Tanner.

He held his hands as though there were nothing to fear from me, so I shot two lefts into his face, and would have thrown a right, only he hit me with a right hook to the body that sent me backward. My God, I thought. A right hook for a lead. A pure brawler for sure. I faked another left that brought a right sizzling just past my nose, followed by his left, a quick, short, lethal punch that just missed. So that was how it would go: I'd punch, and he'd counter with hooks. His arms were too short for anything else, but he was strong enough to kill me with either hand.

I kept throwing lefts into his face, then rights, then combinations— left right left, left right left—and was scoring well, but his countering was vicious and painful. He concentrated on my ribs and upper arms, trying to bash me until my hands would fall too low for a decent defense. He didn't give a damn for the punches he was absorbing, and I wasn't hurting him. As the bell rang to end the first round, I gave him a right lead to the nose that came all the way from my shoes. I might as well have hit him with a feather. He just turned away and sat down on his stool, alone.

In the corner Tommy pulled my mouthpiece and sponged me with ice water. I could see the referee, or whatever he was, lodged against the ropes. Whatever happened, he would be no help. Finally, as the bell rang, Tommy said, "Left lead, then right uppercut, and guard yourself."

Tanner waited until I'd reached center-ring before he rose. I'd reddened his face, but no amount of punching could damage the ruin of his nose. My advantage, if I had one, was reach, not height: punching down is difficult, and I'd never fought a shorter man. I tried left jabs to see if he'd bite and he did, hard on my body with both hands. After that I faked a left and threw Tommy's uppercut into his face, following it with an identical left that made him wince. I spent the rest of the round trying to duplicate this success, but Tanner learned fast. On my third attempt he made me pay by throwing a chopping right into my liver, and I covered up for the last seconds of the round. As we broke for the corners I could swear I heard him laugh.

Tanner was willing to take two to land one, so Tommy ordered me to throw left jabs from as far away as possible, and to counter with long rights. I looked to my side to find Hank and realized that Tommy had been rubbing my left shoulder, and I hadn't even felt it. Tanner's strategy was working.

In the third round I threw punches at Tanner from as far away as possible, but although that kept his bombs from reaching me, the net result was that my punches were rendered even weaker than before. By round's end Tanner had adapted again, smashing my arms with his hooks and picking off my gloves with his own as they came into range. My ribs were getting a rest, but my arms—meaning my defenses—were beginning to drop. The crafty old bastard was having his way.

Between rounds, Tommy told me to keep it up, but I had already decided to do something else. Tommy only wanted me to last six rounds, to survive, but for what? So that the sole judge, the incompetent referee, could award the fight to Tanner? This was probably the last time I'd ever fight. I wanted to win. I said nothing but stared across the ring.

As the fifth round opened, I could see swelling around Tanner's eyes, and his mouthpiece had turned pink. Not much, but it was something. He stood as before, glaring and crablike, fists apart, waiting to strike.

Tanner was the same fighter, but I wouldn't be: now he would face a left-hander. I switched to a right lead, and cracked him twice with straight lefts before backing away from the hooks that came just after. He was surprised, but I knew he'd adjust quickly. Before the round I'd decided to become every boxer I'd seen, one after another, to prevent Tanner from timing my punches and following them home with his hooks. Back and forth from right to left-hander, I hit him a good dozen times before he could fire, all nice solid shots to the face that stung. He was angry and hurting and we both knew his only way out was to force me into the ropes and hammer me inside. Suddenly he lurched forward, bent over, throwing hooks like a reaper. By the time my back hit the ropes I was another boxer, bent lower than he, throwing uppercuts into the gap between his punches. He'd slowed down, but I hadn't. I took a couple to the body but gave his face hell.

Behind me, Tommy was yelling for me to get out, and I did, just as Tanner caught on to the game. He lurched toward me, but I spun away, leaving him nothing. There was only one trick left to pull. I would become Tanner. He crabbed toward me and threw a sweeping right, but I loaded up and hooked hard into his ear, then as he turned away, hooked again to his head with everything I had. Tanner winced and covered up, then swiped at his eye with a glove. His right brow was cut and the blood was in his eye. Knowing his time was running out, Tanner took a few hard-grunting breaths and came at me like a locomotive; like a fool I stood put and tried to match him straight up. For the last thirty seconds of the round we stood toe-to-toe, an old man and a young fool, throwing the hardest blows we could find the strength for. I'd just thrown a right cross into his teeth when his right hand came around like a sling and crashed into my cheek. I hit the canvas seat-first as the bell rang, and watched from a dream as Tanner trod drunkenly back to his corner.

I made it back to the stool with some help, despite ringing in my ears and a toothache that broadcast its pain from my upper jaw. Tommy settled down in front of me, pushing a towel into my face. When he pulled it away, a red rivulet ran off my cheek and onto my knees. There was a roaring that might have been the crowd, but there were so many sounds in my head it was hard to tell. Tommy was talking but I couldn't hear. Then there was something cold on my neck and then I heard, clearly, "Mack, you've got the old man whipped. His hand is broken. Get in there and finish him. The fight is yours."

It was true. Across the ring sat Tanner, brow still bleeding, grimacing as he flexed a right hand that must have shattered against my head in the furious exchange at the end of the fifth. He looked over at me with an expression that seemed to say 'So what? Have you seen your face?'

Then the bell rang and somebody, probably Hank, hoisted me from behind and pushed me forward. At the last second Tommy thumbed some stuff onto my cheek that burned like hell but cleared most of the fog away. With nobody to hoist him, Tanner rose slowly and made his way to the center of the ring. Once there he paused, extending a glove, which I jabbed softly before setting up to fight. He expected me to circle left, into his dim eye and useless hand. Instead I circled right, luring him with distant jabs and faked punches. He had to fight me now, hand or no, find some way to knock me out or make me quit. I wasn't going to go to his blind side, but I wasn't going to lose, either. He kept the right hand up near his ear and threw the left after my punches. I followed him home three times with hard rights, then burned lefts in his side.

Hurt but not finished, he reached back for a last trick, shuffling back to the ropes before my pursuit. Suddenly he sprang forward, threw an arm behind my head and slammed my cheek with his elbow. The pain shot through me and made my face run red again. Enraged, I wrestled him back into the corner and with my shoulder against him hammered lefts into his face, then as he covered up, used both hands against his body. Bent over, he tried to force me away, but I drove him back with Tommy's uppercuts, and, with a leg between his, was thrashing a defenseless man when the bell sounded to end the fight. The referee sauntered out of a neutral corner to raise my hand, which ruined the evening for quite a few bettors.

There wasn't time to savor glory, nor much to savor. The next bout began seconds after we left the ring. Hank steered me outside to the loading dock where I lay, watching the stars spin until Tommy brought the car around. An hour later I was at the Naval Hospital looking one-eyed at my reflection in a towel dispenser as a corpsman laid out sutures. Later I would read in my medical record: "Subject brought in by friends, insists he fell off bicycle—if true, did so after terrific beating." For two weeks I looked awful, and enjoyed it immensely. Some years later a dentist informed me that Tanner had broken my cheekbone. Good for him.

Two months down the road I was discharged from the Navy. Tommy had gone to another command, and Hank— well, Hank married his girl-friend out of necessity and headed off to Seattle, never to reach the big time.

I spent my last month in the service at the transit barracks, pulling shore patrol duty for six hours every other night. One evening I came across two drunken sailors swinging at each other on the sidewalk outside the downtown YMCA. I waited until one had put the other on the pavement, then strode up and said "Okay Sport, clear out, the fight's over." At this the victor faced me, drew a breath—and headed off down Broadway. I didn't even lose my hat.

The Angler

Michael McGrorty

Nineteen forty-seven was a good year to be an American, and a great time to be going to UCLA on the G.I. Bill. I was carrying a load of five classes, two of which were no problem and the others only a bit of work. I was a 22-year-old freshman, there with lots of other service vets. The only difference was that I lived with my folks a few miles away while they stayed in dorms. I had a job too, which meant money for a car and some minor amusements. Not a bad setup, and I knew it.

I remember it was a Monday, which meant Political Science, American History, and four hours of clerking in a store. I sat down in Poli Sci and waited for the class to fill. There was one blank space on the roll sheet. The same thing happened in History. After school I had two hours to kill before work. I drove down Venice Boulevard to see about the guy who'd missed the classes because he was a friend of mine. There was a coffee shop along the strand, a little dump with Italianate columns and outside tables. It was supposed to look like Naples. I got a cup of regular and took it outside, expecting to find somebody. I wasn't disappointed.

He was exactly as old as I was, wearing the mandatory uniform of pressed slacks and sports shirt. I sat at his table and said "If you can't handle hangovers you shouldn't be in the Air Corps." He smiled and said "You get the notes?"

"Always," I said, "but you're down to your last absence."

He waved that off. "Ah, to hell with that. It's boring anyway."

He never did like to be bored. We were raised more or less together in the same West Side L.A. neighborhood, back when it was almost like a country village. We went to the same elementary school, the same middle school, and the same high school. We smoked our first cigarette together;

drank the first beer and threw it up in the same empty lot; swapped clothes and lies and helped each other where we were weak—he in Spanish and me in math; defended one-another and, in a hot spasm of patriotism, joined the army right after Pearl Harbor, and became pilots, because, well, pilots were the guys to be.

After the war we came home: Jim Crews to his people and me to my own. We signed up for college and went off, taking all the same classes but one, his math being far ahead of mine. Civilian life was odd after the war. We'd danced a swift, crazy jitterbug for a chunk of our lives, then were dropped like a phonograph needle onto a very sweet, slow waltz. It was harder for Jim to take. He was the one who would ride the hood of a car down Wilshire, or rent a yellow tux for the prom. I was the stamp collector, the one who kept a careful diary in which nothing much happened. For years I was the string to his balloon.

In the Air Corps he would have finished first in training except for his stunts. He was a natural flier; I had to learn everything and practice. What he did he did like an animal, from instinct. Still, he was the best pilot I ever saw.

I stirred some cream into my coffee and wondered "Do you think they'll ever fly people around the way they ship them on trains? That would be something. Plenty of jobs for pilots."

He gave me a portion of his grin and said "It's like this, old buddy. People are flying today. Over at Mines Field you can catch a plane to any-where. But it costs plenty. You got to compete with air mail, and probably will for a long time. What's that, a nickel an ounce? They'd have to charge you a hundred fifty bucks to make that up, and they can't pack you in as tight. The birds got to get larger, cheaper to fly. There's a break point to every situation. Right now the two curves are too far apart. I'd give it ten years at the least."

"You think you could fly them?"

"I could fly a stagecoach through Stalin's bunghole, but nobody's going to let me. Come on, let's get a beer."

It was only one o'clock, but Venice had a slew of beer-and-wine joints that opened at six in the morning. We turned in to one, had them pull a pitcher, and sat down near a window to enjoy it. As usual, Jim did more of the enjoying.

The world had never seen an experiment like aviation during the war. The government took thousands of men whose only qualifications were good eyesight and fair reflexes, and handed them extremely expensive, inherently dangerous vehicles to aim through the skies at high speed. Quality control for the hardware was tight; for the humanity much less so. There were very few perfect pilots in the Army Air Corps. Jim and I had our flaws—he was highly skilled but not terribly careful; I was careful but not highly skilled.

They put us to flying P-47s, but we weren't shooting down German fighters. Our job was softening up France for the invasion, and we made it pretty soft, if the aerial photos were any indication. It wasn't too long before we could navigate from the ruins we'd created and were running out of things to bomb and strafe near the coast.

In the winter months we would go fishing for Bonito at Santa Monica. You found a ledge with a good drop-off, cast into the hole and reel back to see what luck gave you. We kept a fire going in a lard can and would grill the first one we caught. As with everything else, Jim was better than me. I think he caught three to my one, and he could get them when nobody else did. He'd take a run toward the surf like a javelin thrower, tossing the long bamboo rod forward at the last moment, letting the line unspool as the weight arched over the breakers. When I did that, I looked like a man trying to kill a housefly with a broom. There were Japanese fish shops in town that bought all we could catch. Sometimes we'd end up with five or ten dollars. Jim always split down the middle, though I almost never caught as many.

Everybody knows now that the invasion landed in Normandy. What they don't remember is that there was a great deal of faking beforehand. They had us flying around, doing reconnaissance and hitting targets from Spain to Belgium. The idea was to keep the Nazis from concentrating in any one area, and it worked. Aside from that, we were wrecking a lot of their offensive capacity, which meant that no matter where we landed, there'd be fewer of them to oppose us.

Occasionally they'd take us in and tell us we had a 'special target' that day. Usually this was based on information from the French Underground, and usually meant railroad targets or tank movements. One day in April of '44, we got briefed about a particular target to the east of Amiens that the intelligence service said of was of "extremely high value." They briefed us for half a day, saying that the Germans were gathering field officers for a conference on defensive preparations. It was to be a two-day affair, held in a seized chapel and school. The officers were to be brought to the site in separate cars, dressed as civilians, under cover of night; their departure would be in darkness as well. They expected at least two hundred to be present—quite a bag if we could hit it at the right moment.

Our squadron knew the area and was split into parts for the operation: six to create a diversion to the north, as the Germans would be expecting our regular forays, and the remaining three to perform the real attack. Jim would be the flight leader, making the initial run; I would make the second, and our third, Cole Jackson, would be the sweeper. We'd carry two 500-pound bombs apiece—not an unusual load, and more than enough to pulverize the buildings.

From the photos it seemed that the school and chapel were right along the Somme, in the midst of flat cropland. Our route would follow the river all the way from the ocean—about sixty miles from the sea to the target. The way back would be by compass heading or 'best possible' if there was heavy flak or fighters. We would be on the Germans' radar the whole time, from takeoff in England to return landing. Our defense consisted of flying low, flying fast, and having a lot of diversions in the air. Apart from that, the Nazis were quite low on air power—if we got shot down it would be from the ground.

The night before the raid, Jim got a serious look on his face and said to me, "I just wanted to tell you one thing, in case I ever get killed: the only way you're going to get Bonito is by casting over your head. You're trying to do it sidearm." That was what passed for a solemn pronouncement from him.

We took off just at dawn, with clouds scudding across the English countryside and dragging the channel north-to-south. Our target was supposed to be in clean air but the last forecast was for 50% cover and a thousand-foot ceiling. If we hadn't been in a tight window for time the thing would have been called off.

Our second group tailed off and rode high over the coastline before crossing into the country near Dieppe. They would have been spreading out there, making shadows on the radar to occupy the watchers. At the same time, our three swept in low at the mouth of the Somme, happy for once to be hidden from the flak guns by the tumbling clouds. They would know we were around about the time we left for home.

Ahead of me, Jim slid along the river's path like a race car driver taking turns on a road course. The land was tremendously green and lush near the river, like a piece of Ireland. None of us who flew there ever came away without wishing to see the place some day without risking his life.

Just before Amiens the clouds collapsed upon the landscape, obscuring the town and our path to the target. It was enough that we knew to head straight west when the buildings passed beneath us. After that we counted seconds and waited for the sign.

Five minutes and thirty seconds from the spire of Amiens' cathedral, Jim would release his bombs, dropping by sight; five seconds later I would drop my own, followed by the last raider. The delayed fuses would twiddle their electric thumbs for a few moments, then the whole affair would be wrecked—buildings, Nazis, and all.

We were about a minute from drop when I lost Jim in the vapor. He'd been going in and out of the cover but now there was no 'out' and I could do nothing but maintain course. I had very little height but dropped a bit lower, finding the four loops of the Somme but no flight leader—and nobody flying behind me. We were in radio silence and I felt helpless, but the plan was to make a single pass and head home, regardless of result. Besides that, I knew that Jim was the best navigator on earth and would surely find the target.

Without my guide, I was reluctant to make a choice from among the scattered landmarks along the stream. I counted the turns of the river; when I got to four, I figured that I'd passed my chance for a shot and that Jim had dropped and was waiting for results. Sure enough, in a tight loop of the waters, a pair of orange blasts cut through the shadowy daylight—

one of us had hit the spot. I turned to the homeward heading, gave it military throttle and waited for the coastline to appear. On the way I let my two five-hundred pounders go for a swim, unarmed.

England appeared right where God put it. I rode the beach until the turning place, went inland and discovered my two friends a bit downrange. Jim set down first and we followed, rolling to a halt near the maintenance hangar and the photo shack.

The colonel asked us "How'd it go," and Jim said "I put them right in the barrel. Lucky I caught a hole in the clouds."

The film backed up his claim. It showed one bomb falling just before the foundation of the school, and the second right before the chapel. That meant that they exploded beneath or within—a ruinous result. We had a nice dinner and were toasting our success in the base pub when an MP came bustling into the place, calling out our names. He gathered us up like errant schoolboys, drove to the CO's office and shoved us inside.

The Old Man wore a nasty look. He wasted no time.

"That job you did today. You hit the wrong buildings."

Jim replied "Not possible. Look at the gun camera."

The nasty look turned to anger. "We got two reports from the French. The buildings you hit were a girls' school. You killed about thirty civilians. The French are outraged—the command is furious. Consider yourselves confined to quarters until this is resolved."

In the barracks Jim said to me "There's no way in hell I hit the wrong buildings. It's right in a turn of the river—brick, chimney-pots, surrounded by trees. Just like in the recon photos. Something's wrong here."

He went to sleep, but I went to the intel office to have a look at the photos. There was our target, surrounded by a twist of river. Brick; chimney pots; trees. I pulled out surrounding shots taken within a kilometer of the place. There, within another bend of the Somme was another pair of brick buildings, nearly identical—with chimney pots, surrounded by a tall hedge of trees. Nobody had shown us the other pictures, only those of the target. At our speed they had been about eight seconds apart. Eight seconds, in cloudy weather, on exactly the same course heading.

In the summer of our fifteenth year, Jim and I rented a pair of ocean kayaks at the Malibu pier for a fishing trip in the kelp beds. Instead of rods we brought spears—steel tridents with barbed ends, especially good for getting Yellowtail and Sea Bass. The end piece was connected to a reel of line; your fish ran with that and you reeled it in, hand over hand. This called for lightning reflexes; you made up your mind and tossed in less than a second. The idea was to hit right behind the head.

As usual, Jim was holding a clinic in the subject while I was just fumbling along. I had only one in my creel and he was almost at the limit when his eyes got big and he threw down with all his might. He yelled "It's a bass—real big one." There was a lot of thrashing between our two kayaks, and then the fish headed for the bottom. Jim gave it a few seconds before hauling in. There were a lot of bubbles and blood in the water. The final yank revealed his prize—a harbor seal, pinned right through the skull.

I remember his mouth fell open and he said "No" over and over. He turned away, and I had to yank the barbs from the animal's head. It tumbled down through the water, trailing blood as it fell to the seafloor. We paddled back to the dock, gave away our fish, and waited for the bus in silence. Sitting in the rearmost seats, he said to me "Christ, man, I killed a seal. A seal. That's so wrong." When we got to his house, he tipped up his father's bottle of scotch, swallowed a huge dose, and mumbled "I'm never going to get over this." I don't know if he did, and we never spoke of it again.

They held what they called an Official Enquiry, after which we sat on our hands awaiting a decision. In the end they issued a Statement, which read in part:

"This Board finds that the bombing of the girl's school outside Amiens was the result of an error on the part of the command to provide adequate instruction and direction to the assigned pilots, especially with regard to the presence of a practically identical pair of buildings in the near vicinity."

Three officers in our Intelligence wing were sacked, and the affair was officially over. It took three months to resolve; the war had about a year until its end. But neither of us ever flew for the Air Corps again. I got promoted to fill one of the vacated intelligence positions, and Lieutenant James Adams Crews began to come apart.

Our division had by this time made the jump across to France, and taken on new fliers. Jim was given a lot of paperwork that he studiously neglected while recuperating from hangovers. After a while the command got tired of this and called him to account; he was either to straighten out or be sent back to the states on a medical discharge. He managed to slow it down enough to pass for normal, and soldiered on through the last months of the conflict. At one point he took a three-day pass, ostensibly to see Paris. I knew he was lying the way you'd know your mother's voice. But he went, to Paris, or wherever.

I figured the MPs would bring him back in a straitjacket, but on the fourth morning he appeared, calm, shaven, and alert, eating his pancakes as if he'd only gone to post a letter. We avoided the subject until the end of the meal, when he said "Let's go for a walk."

I let him carry the load. He said "I was down a ways, stealing rides from the infantry. Got along one or two of the rivers. You know what? They got trout in there. Browns and Brookies. I think they're brought from England, back God knows how many eons. There were old men and boys fishing with hand lines and straight poles—no reels to speak of. Like something out of the 18th Century. No lures. All bait, mostly grubs."

I asked him, "Did you try your hand?"

"Yeah. There was a man, old fellow, named Arnaud. Spoke decent English. He showed me. He was tying his line to a tree branch and letting the bobber float downstream. Almost no current. It's not really fishing—you just wait. He got a couple strikes and then hooked a sucker that he cut for bait. Diagonal strip of skin, on the bias like a pork belly, but really thin. Rubbed it in the guts and tossed it down. Got himself a Brownie for the pan."

"What was the hook," I asked.

He turned away, twisted his wristwatch and replied "I bet you think I went, Andy. Sure, you thought I went."

"I didn't think you went there. I thought you went to Paris to get loaded."

"I did. But that was because—because I didn't have the guts to go."

That Jim didn't have the guts to do something was nearly as amazing a thing to me as that he would admit it.

I said "Okay, so you didn't go. That was the idea for the whole trip? Just that?"

He looked at his hands as if there was something in them that would explain, but said "I was hiking down the river, you know, figuring to find the place, but I had to quit for the day and when the sun came up I lost my nerve. After that I hooked a ride to Paris and hit the champagne."

"And so what now? You done with it?"

He swallowed—once, twice—in the way he did when he was about to cut loose with an idea. "Andy, I want to go. I really do. But you got to come with me."

I said "You didn't tell me what the hook was."

He said "Oh hell, it was wider than long—rusty—way too big for trout. Probably the only one he had."

"But it worked."

"Oh yeah. Now tell me you're going with me, Andy."

"Okay, I'll go. Next weekend. I'll drive. But you promise me something. You won't touch a drop until we head back."

He agreed, and I didn't believe him.

It wasn't easy to get the jeep, but I called in a lot of markers and stole the gas besides. It was only fifty miles to the outskirts of Amiens, but the road wasn't in good shape and it took us four hours. The last part we did by dead reckoning, just as if we'd been flying over to drop a load. At the end, our road passed through a long tunnel of poplars that wound along the river until the trees ended in a flat expanse of fallow ground. It might have passed for a harvested field except for the neat piles of bricks that rested between the field and the river's edge. Bricks that had been the walls of a school and church.

There were two long rectangles of raw brown soil there. The first we came to would have been the chapel. There was no foundation; even that had been removed. The flagstone paths to the side and rear doors angled from the gravel lane to nowhere, now. The trees that had shaded the building were gone as well, their stumps pulled away for firewood.

Jim went ahead to the school building site. It was half-again larger, wide enough for classrooms and some offices. There too the stone walkways angled dutifully toward entrances which no longer existed. I watched him walk around its perimeter, shoes pressing prints into the damp earth. At the far side, closest to the river, he sat on one of the stacks of bricks, arms around his knees like a small boy. I left him there for a while, turning away toward the broad expanse of farmland, broken here and there by the line of the roadway and small stands of trees.

It might have been a half hour later when I heard him call my name. He was still on the stacked bricks, holding one—a corner piece, more like a tile, blackened on one angle.

"Here, look," he said. "this was from a stairway. Must be a hundred years old."

We sat there talking about bricks and mortar and old French buildings for a while, until Jim said "Andy, do you think they can hear us?"

I said "I don't know."

We drove away, this time toward the west, into a little village where Jim thought we could get some lunch. We bought a bottle of water, some cheese and bread from a little shop whose keeper informed us that he was very happy not to be under the Germans because they didn't always pay the right price and were moreover arrogant. We ate outside under the eaves of the shop, Jim slicing cheese and bread like a man cutting bait.

The shop owner appeared, bringing with him a small cake and two forks. "Here," he said, "a gift for the liberation."

Jim replied "What happened to the church and school over there?"

The shop owner pursed his lips and said "It was bombed by mistake. The Americans apologized and paid money to the families."

I said "What will happen to the school—to the land?"

"It is owned by a religious order. The girls' school was there, and the school for boys a kilometer or so away. They will build another school, I think."

When the man went away I could see Jim getting that look in his eye—the one that came before a few too many drinks. There was nothing I could do; he'd lived up to his promise, so I let him buy a big jug of wine, which we split, two-and-one, some at the little shop and the rest on the road back to the airfield.

I noticed that something had gone away from him since the accident. Jim used to be one of those guys who drank and felt good. Now he seemed to drink without any improvement at all. Whatever place the alcohol was hitting, it wasn't the 'happy' button.

About that time they started consolidating the Air Corps, and our squadron vanished into history. Jim and I got orders to England, and then, just when the Germans gave in, to the States; they thought we were going to have to deal with the Japanese, but then that came to an end and we just went back to Los Angeles, and college, and the rest.

Our first pitcher of beer led to another, and I had to call my boss to tell him about a flat tire. The day fell away gradually, until we watched the sun set from the high tide line while passing a pint of cheap bourbon back and forth, taking small sips so it would last.

He said, "I want to try one of those glass-fiber rods one of these days. I hear they whip like hell."

"Don't buy it," I said. "Rent one first. Never know if you're going to like it."

A shark cleaved the momentary space between two swells and he said "That was a Leopard. Sucking in the halibut."

The breeze came up from offshore and it got too cold to be there without a jacket. I was about to say we should head back when Jim said "I'm going to quit, Andy. There's nothing in it for me."

I had been waiting for that and said "You quit college and I'll kill you. God damn it Jim, what the hell are you thinking?"

He handed me the last swig and said "Sitting in stupid rooms all day listening to some idiot talk about history or politics. What the hell do they know? I'm just tired of it."

I came around to sit between him and the glow of the horizon, pointed my finger at his face and said "Listen, you've been in the crapper since the thing with the girls' school in France. Listen to me now: but for a few clouds in the wrong place, it could have been me dropping on them, or the other guy—any of us. Apart from that, how many civilians do you think we blew to hell on those trains we hit, or the stations? And what about the misses? You know damned right well those killed civilians, too."

He poked at the sand with a finger and asked "So, you got no regrets?"

"Sure, I got regrets. I regret going into the service altogether. You think you hate school? I'm 23 years old, in English classes I could have passed when I was 16, and I got more years of that ahead of me. I won't have a decent teaching job until I finish graduate school, if then. You remember, I didn't have to go. I could have pulled the single-son deferment and that job in the aircraft plant."

"Well why the hell did you do it?"

I could have strangled him. "I did it, old friend, because of you. You were the one who was so crazy to be a pilot. I did it because you did, because I wanted to be with you. I almost flunked out. I would have if you weren't there. You wouldn't go in if I didn't, and I couldn't stay in if you weren't there. That's the story. So if you think I'm going to let you bug out of college now, you may as well jump off the pier."

A week later he quit school. In retrospect I should have realized that, accident or not, Jim wasn't built right for college—for the book learning, quiet listening routine. You missed three classes under the G.I. Bill, you were out—and he was.

I let him spool out his line for a while, until I got a call from a guy at an aircraft company asking if I could come out and test fly a plane for him. I said I would, but gathered up Jim and brought him out to Torrance to fly the thing. It was more or less an improvement on the P-38; Jim looped it a couple of times over Palos Verdes, spun it around Catalina, and the wings stayed on. The company signed him to a contract that involved very little more than taking planes up in the air for a few hours every week and then telling engineers what was wrong with them. Within a couple of years Jim was making pretty good money, with enough time to fish like hell wherever he wanted.

I graduated and was in my first teaching job when Korea blew up. They were desperate for pilots and both Jim and I were still of draft age. I lucked out because my eyes fell below the standard, but Jim's liver had enough miles left on it for another run.

The Angler

He wrote me:

What a mess this is. Andy, what we're doing here is just about murder, and I don't mean just of soldiers. The civilian deaths here are atrocious. This isn't France or Germany. This is a civil war, no matter what you read about Communism. The people have nowhere to run; they're pressed from all sides. It's an ugly war in an ugly place and hard to find the good guy.

I'm flying P-51s now—converted to attack planes, which is a terrible mistake, and you know why. The coolant system is exposed and ground fire brings them down easily. We're losing planes like moths in a fireplace. It's a shame because most of them got through the last one only to be sent over here. It seems like the 20th Century will be all wars, doesn't it?

Three weeks later I got a call from Jim's sister. He'd been shot down leading an attack on troop formations. There wasn't any doubt; the plane had been hit and gone down without a sign of a parachute. The best friend of my entire life was gone, forever.

It was the week of winter break. I took out my surf pole, cut a strip of bait and spent a night on the beach trying to do a decent overhead cast. The moon came out, danced atop the ridges above Malibu, and I drank until I couldn't feel the cold surf on my legs. At last I hooked something heavy; it ran with the current but I caught it turning toward shore and reeled for all it was worth. In the silvery moonlight I could see it was a Bonito, large and brilliant, played to a standstill. I pulled the hook and watched him turn again into the waves.

Made in the USA
San Bernardino, CA
14 January 2020

62900291R00090